How To Have A Good Life After You're Dead

Explorations Into The Afterlife
A Modern Book Of The Dead

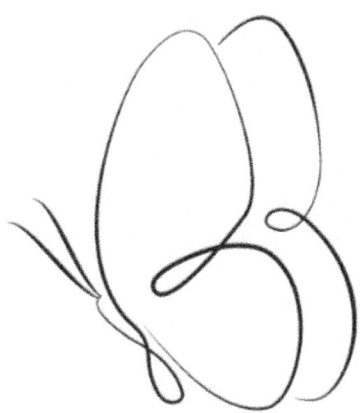

MIKE MARABLE

MIKE MARABLE

Kindness

Service

Empathy

Love

HOW TO HAVE A GOOD LIFE AFTER YOU'RE DEAD

Copyright Owner: Mike Marable

All rights reserved. No part of this publication may be reproduced, distributed, or transmitted in any form or by any means, including photocopying, recording, or other electronic or mechanical methods, without the prior written permission of the publisher, except in the case of brief quotations embodied in critical reviews and certain other noncommercial uses permitted by copyright law.

Permission Requests, write to the publisher, addressed "Attention: Permissions Coordinator." at the address below.
3 Woodbridge Ct.
Trabuco Canyon, CA 92679
Author Website: mikemarable.com

ISBN: 978-1-961636-39-2 (Paperback)
ISBN: 978-1-961636-40-8 (eBook)

Library of Congress Control Number: 2023923506

First printing edition 2023

Blue Mount Publishers
5670 Wilshire Blvd,
Los Angeles, CA 90036

MIKE MARABLE

I would rather have questions that can't be answered than answers that can't be questioned.

-Richard Feynman, Physicist

INTRODUCTION

G. Scott Sparrow, PhD

I had the privilege of meeting Mike Marable almost 40 years ago in Virginia Beach, where I worked at the Association for Research and Enlightenment. Like so many people who are awakening to powerful, spiritual realities, he wasn't sure what was happening to him. I was able to confirm that his experiences were no less than kundalini awakenings—profound transformative experiences known and honored in the East but not well understood in our own culture. I sensed then that he was on the verge of doing great things since people who have such awakenings thereafter possessed increased faculties for non-material experiences. And now, many years later, Mike Marable may know as much about the afterlife as anyone probably can from our vantage point here having the human experience. He has the skill of being able to assist souls in the transition from this world to the next and thus has a unique and invaluable perspective that will benefit all of us. His book will reassure those of us whose loved ones have passed and will help the rest of us approach the end of our lives with positive anticipation.

MIKE MARABLE

Scott Sparrow, Ed.D., dream researcher, psychotherapist, and author of Lucid Dreaming: Dawning of the Clear Light.

HOW TO HAVE A GOOD LIFE AFTER YOU'RE DEAD

FOREWORD

Hardly a week goes by when Mike and I are not in contact, reporting on our exploits in the non-physical universe, comparing notes, or sounding each other out about certain out-of-body experiences (OBE) related to our perception of reality. This has happened for a few years, and we have even videotaped our conversations. What makes our exchange so valuable to me is that Mike is not only a very experienced OBE explorer of the afterlife state but also a man who has both feet on the ground, is rational, sober, and analytical, not at all prone to unproven theories or beliefs. He is very reluctant to derive a set conclusion from his experiences. If we explore a subject such as the afterlife state, it is incredibly important to avoid falling victim to assumptions, beliefs, and theories, and we both agree that the only thing that counts is personal experience and its reporting. This is the only way to find and crystalize a consensus by independently having similar experiences. In the end, there is a statistical component which will bring us a little bit closer to proving that the afterlife state is a fact. We as an individual awareness, transition from a state of physical identification to one of non-physical.

It is indistinguishable for people who go through the transition process.

OBE travelers all agree on how difficult it can be to determine which state you are in, and we employ a variety of methods to determine whether we are awake in the physical world or awake in the non-physical because the feeling of being aware and awake is identical. The environments we find ourselves in are also very much the same. Some people use their fingers and see if they can poke them through their hands. I personally use the "hover test" to rise into the air to figure out what my current stratum of consciousness is. Even when we return from our OBE journeys and wake up in our beds or the meditation chair, we are not necessarily assured that we are back in the physical reality and may be in yet another non-physical state termed a false awakening.

Dead people don't fare much better. Many of the thousands of people who die every day and leave this planet behind with their bodies buried or cremated have no idea what has happened to them. It is the sad state of our materialist culture that we hardly pay any attention to the reality everybody will inevitably experience. Apart from vague and outdated religious beliefs, there is very little in our education system or culture that prepares us for life ahead after we die. The prevailing attitude is, "When I am gone, I am gone". However, that is not the reality; we are not gone when we are gone. Quite the opposite—most of us will only just come alive after a life of struggle, illness, and hardship, especially those who are better informed.

The fact that the afterlife territories are overcrowded with uninformed people has been the driving force in my own reporting of these experiences, where I have studied in great detail what this new reality entails over many years and hundreds of hours of exploration. However, Mike has taken his experiences to a completely new level. Not only has he explored and investigated these territories during countless OBEs, but he has also made it his task to help people on "The Other Side" who got stranded and have no idea how to find their way around or progress further to their natural home, which of course is in the much higher states of consciousness, where we find true liberation from our ignorance, which many near-death experiencers categorize as their true home.

Instead of soaring straight into the home state, Mike has made it his mission, first and foremost, to help those who are stranded in the darker realms. I detect in Mike an aspect of the Bodhisattva, who vowed first to help those unhappy souls find their way out of the darkness before he feels happy to move up into the undoubtedly more pleasurable regions of the higher dimensions. But it is exactly this need to be of service to others that distinguishes him and is a clear sign of his moral and ethical integrity.

When I first read this manuscript, it quickly became obvious what an important book this is. It's one of a kind that I am aware of. The subtitle spells it out: *A Modern Book of the Dead*.

It's a long overdue guidebook for all of us, in my opinion, because nobody will escape the inevitable journey ahead of us.

Mike and I are both travelers on a mission. I knew very soon that my mission was to shed light on areas yet unknown to many. Mike, on the other hand was given, right from the very beginning, the task to help those poor folks who get stranded in the twilight regions. This makes his work of invaluable importance in this time of ignorance. He picks up lost strugglers and even whole groups of people, sometimes numbering dozens and escorts them toward the light where they make their transition into their home state. If you are like me, not only will you thoroughly enjoy this book, but you will also receive powerful instructions to help you cross the dividing line when your time comes to leave your body behind.

-Jurgen Ziewe

HOW TO HAVE A GOOD LIFE AFTER YOU'RE DEAD

DEDICATION

I want to thank Gayla, my partner of nineteen years, for listening to my strange tales and never flinching or judging. I also thank my best friend Hunter for lying beside me, keeping me company as I wrote this book and never complaining.

I love you both and without you nothing would be as good.

MIKE MARABLE

CONTENTS

INTRODUCTION	5
FOREWORD	7
DEDICATION	11
How This Book Came About	13
Philosophy and Science Struggle to Understand Consciousness	25
Living With a Foot In Both Worlds	37
OBEs and Portals to Other Dimensions	53
What Do I Need to Know Before I Leave	69
Choosing A Good Death	84
I See Dead People (and try to lend them a helping hand)	108
Retrievals And Other Experiences	114
The Earth Experience Is a Hot Ticket	183
My Best Assessment	194
Epilogue	196
Author	201

How This Book Came About

The book you are now reading has the audacity to dig deep into one of the biggest questions most of us probably will consider at some point in our lives; *what happens when we die?* You may think you already have a good idea. It may be that this book won't alter those beliefs much; then again, it could. We use terms such as death and the afterlife to communicate with each other about the line between our physical and non-physical existence.

The reality is that life is a continuation. You could say that we are as dead as we are ever going to be right now.

Your consciousness is an energy that cannot cease to exist; it only changes its state. Consider water for example and the states it can occupy. Ice and steam have the same atomic structure but are in different states that are influenced by the rate of vibration of the particles. Think of yourself as like ice while in your physical form and steam when you die. You simply shift the frequency. Like changing from one station to another on the radio. The reality we go to when we die is all around us. Our physical equipment is efficiently designed to allow us to experience this reality only when we are in a body and awake. When we sleep or enter certain altered states of consciousness, we can access other frequencies.

My larger aim for writing this book is to assist people in preparation for what one might term a "good death." This involves taking steps in advance of that moment to ensure that your preferences and decisions are communicated clearly to your family and caregivers. You also want to be prepared in other ways involving closure and not leave it for the last days of a lingering illness. This book will hopefully help reduce some of the stress that can accompany your transition, both before and after you've moved on. Think of this as a modern version of previous books of the dead in that its goal is to present ways for people to navigate post-physical life and ensure the best possible outcome.

One thing is certain, everyone reading this will go through this experience. It is something we all have in common.

How much do you really know about what happens after you take your last physical breath? I am going to share what I have learned through thirty-plus years of traveling into some of the regions we might occupy after we transition out of physical life. I go to these places via a process called an out-of-body experience. Sometimes, using this altered state of consciousness, I assist people who get stuck in the lower frequency levels close to the Earth's environment. Some people don't want to move on. It's my opinion that the overwhelming majority of people who die have a very smooth and beautiful transition experience. There are also those who are either reluctant or don't realize that something happened to them. This information is not intended to alarm people, just to be aware that that for some this does happen. When it does the experience can be more difficult. There are reasons why some individuals don't move on, and these are unrelated to a person's character or value.

One example is an attachment to certain people and circumstance in the life just lived. Another is fear of what might be waiting for them, possibly some form of judgment. I offer some suggestions for how to successfully move into the next reality.

My travels into the levels of post-human life that are available after death are not dreams, fantasies, or an overly active imagination, as some might assume. They are as real as anything we encounter in physical reality. That materialist science has not yet proven that out-of-body abilities exist is not something that concerns me. I have been doing this several times a week since 1987, and I know what I experience and how to differentiate them from dreams. Universities around the world conduct research on psychical phenomena and have discovered substantial anecdotal evidence supporting out-of-body experiences, telepathy, and the existence of something beyond death. These have been collected, reported on, and written up in prestigious journals. There are thousands of books that have been written on these topics. Millions of people report these experiences. We should be able to confidently declare that consciousness is not limited to the brain, and when we die, that it is not the end. It's the beginning of something else. Something new.

It may help to think of me as a kind of travel agent who volunteers to assist people in their transition from one reality system to another. I am offering suggestions on how to have a better experience when you find yourself waking up in another world one day. My goal is for you to contemplate the advantages of shedding as much baggage as possible and acquiring comprehensive knowledge about these distant lands. I strongly encourage you to achieve this through your own personal experiences and strive to become at ease with these regions that will eventually be part of your next stage of reality.

The information you find here, and through your own explorations, may help you effectively navigate around once you get there. It won't be as foreign a land as you might think.

If you are counting on a religious-style heaven with angels, you can certainly have that, for a while at least. Your ideal may be the universe's most luxurious Ritz Carlton-style resort on a beautiful

HOW TO HAVE A GOOD LIFE AFTER YOU'RE DEAD

sea. Others may want to bypass these extravagant movie sets and start the process of digging into the core nature of reality beyond the façade of illusions. There are fantastic learning opportunities and environments where you can achieve this: universities of knowledge. These are things you can start contemplating immediately, and there are advantages to acting now. Begin by setting an intention and envisioning your ideal outcome for what you want to happen. You can create a storyboard to help plan it out, or you can choose to improvise. These choices are always entirely yours.

If you do decide that you like the idea of being as prepared as possible for your trip to another reality system, there are steps that you can take. This journey is different, of course, because you won't be coming back. When going to another land terrestrially, you want to get familiar with its customs and how things might be different there from what you are used to. The areas we go to after we die are thought-responsive environments. By this, I mean that your emotions, expectations, and thinking have an impact on what you see and experience. As a result, your preparation varies from that of a terrestrial journey. For instance, it proves advantageous to seek closure regarding challenging life experiences. Consider assessing areas where there might be unresolved issues, such as in relationships. You may argue that you are too busy living to think about what happens when you die. This is a reasonable stance.

Every night you have a dry run at death in dreams where

you travel around in these worlds, though you may not remember them. When you are driving, sailing, and flying around in cars, ships, and airplanes, you are traveling. Your mind creates a convenient metaphor for you to relate to these experiences, but in truth you are visiting other realities. Think of all the strange cities you visit and people you interact with, who seem as familiar to you as your own family, yet you have no idea who they are when you wake up.

This happens throughout our lives. It gets accelerated the closer we get to your ultimate departure date. End-of-life care professionals notice that patients in their last days of hospice frequently report dreams about train stations, ship docks, and airports. It is not uncommon to hear from those leaving that they need to pack for their trip. For example, my father got out of bed and started packing his clothes in the days before he left. The one thing we cannot anticipate is the exact departure date. If you left tomorrow, do you feel that you could go with few regrets? Do the people responsible for your estate have what they need to close out your affairs? What's your plan for when you arrive in your new home? Most of us haven't given that last question any thought at all.

In 1987, while I was minding my own business, I had what eminent humanistic psychologist Abraham Maslow called a "peak" experience: an event that permanently altered my perception of what I thought I knew about this world and my own identity. These events are clinically referred to as STEs (spiritually transformative experiences).

The one that most people are familiar with is an NDE (near-death experience). To put it simply, during a NDE, a person may have the experience of leaving their physical body, usually resulting from a sudden traumatic event that stops the heart, and the brain no longer shows any activity. You may be familiar with the work of clinical researchers into the NDE phenomenon, such as doctors Bruce Greyson, Kenneth Ring, Pim Van Lommel, Peter Fenwick, Yvonne Kason and Raymond Moody. These medical professionals have devoted a significant portion of their lives to researching and corroborating the evidence from hundreds of thousands of cases that strongly indicate our survival beyond physical death. This is what we call evidence.

I am fortunate that I didn't have to endure the trauma of almost dying to be able to see these areas that people report on. I started to travel in the OBE state shortly after my experience and regularly continue to have them, often visiting into some of the regions described in NDEs. I also go to other places that are rarely mentioned except by travelers like me. One of those travelers is the person who wrote the forward for this book, Jurgen Ziewe. He and others do this through the very out-of-body phenomenon that is sometimes reported by people who have near-death experiences. You may have heard stories of people floating above their bodies in the hospital emergency room while doctors try to resuscitate them. An out-of-body experience is similar to this phenomenon, with the important distinction that in an OBE the body and brain continue to function while we are asleep in our beds. Some individuals can also encounter this experience during deep meditation. They exit their body while sitting in a chair in a relaxed, altered state of consciousness.

Following my STE, I was left with this ability, or annoyance, depending on how you want to think of it. I would find myself standing in my bedroom looking around and seeing my sleeping body lying in bed. I wasn't unfamiliar with this kind of strangeness because, in college, I read Robert Monroe's book, *Journeys Out of The Body*. Robert Monroe was a businessman living in Ohio who became interested in sleep learning in the 1950s. He cites these sessions as possibly having something to do with his unexpectedly leaving his physical body. I got to meet Mr. Monroe in 1990 and 1991 when I attended some of the programs at his training center in Virginia.

I continue my travels in the tradition of Robert Monroe, Emmanuel Swedenborg, Shamans, and others throughout history who have ventured out beyond the boundaries of physical reality into the lands of the dead. It is an ancient practice. I and others carry on the legacy of visiting these regions and report back to our tribes what we learn so that it might benefit others.

It is an honor to have this skill; to go to the places we

HOW TO HAVE A GOOD LIFE AFTER YOU'RE DEAD

occupy when the earth life has ended. We can bring back information that is universally beneficial. It is a sacred responsibility in my mind. I strive to get it right.

This book was purposefully written so that someone can read the segments in the order they might prefer. It is purposely structured like a collection of essays. Feel free to jump around and read the sections that grab your attention. It's not necessarily a cover-to-cover kind of read unless you prefer to do it that way. There is a lot of information per page; not much of it is fluff out of respect for the reader's time. There are four informal sections. The first is dedicated to background and explanations surrounding how we can access information outside of the limitations of our senses and the physical brain. The second section is dedicated to how to navigate in the world after you leave physical reality and secure the experience of the "good death".

The third section comprises a range of experiences I've had in these realms and my stories of assisting individuals with their transitions. The final section is dedicated to helping the reader comprehend that life is an ongoing journey, and what you do in your current circumstances serves as preparation for all that lies ahead. The human experience is a valuable part of our learning and shouldn't be considered some karmic backwater location where people atone for their mistakes. On the contrary, it is an advanced learning environment and a highly sought-after experience. You are most fortunate to be here.

TERMINOLOGY

There will be concepts and terminology used in this book that the reader may not be familiar with. In an effort to make the material as accessible as possible, I include these terms up front to assist in your reading and to help you understand what I, as the author, mean when I use these words. There are books that go in greater depth on these subjects. I include suggested reading material at the end of the book.

OBE

An out-of-body experience is sometimes referred to as astral projection. They are similar in that a non-physical aspect of the person's multidimensional wholeness is separated from the physical body with conscious awareness and memory of the experience. It often takes place during REM cycles during sleep, and yet people can achieve this state through other means, such as meditation. Without delving too deep into esoteric explanations about what distinguishes it from the physical realm and why it occurs, I'll simply state that it is a natural function that everyone and some animals share.

NDE

The near-death experience is a phenomenon that has been experienced by millions of people. It usually involves a traumatic event in which their heart stops and there is no discernible brain function. This is the clinical definition of death. The reason it is described as "near death" is that the individual maintains their usual waking consciousness throughout the process despite the condition of the body. Some return from these episodes with vivid memories of their experiences. As part of this experience, some people are aware of leaving their physical body and traveling into another dimension of reality where they encounter a variety of situations that seem as real, or even more real, than their physical world.

CONSENSUS REALITIES

People who travel in through an OBE often encounter communities of people who were once living in the physical reality prior to their death. It seems they can enter communities with other like-minded individuals and resume a life that resembles the one they were living in physically or opt for something else. Some of us who travel to these places refer to them as "consensus realities". They can take a variety of themes, appearances, and sizes. Some can look like what we might think of as "heaven". Some look like cities, a small town, or a place out in nature. There seems to be unlimited variety. We discover that individuals are drawn to one of these experiences based on their interests, beliefs, and the frequency of their consciousness.

RETRIEVALS

This is a term (also called "rescues") some use to refer to an act of helping earth-bound people who physically died but haven't made a complete transition toward the light. It could be that they are afraid to go or don't know they have died. People like me can help them access the necessary vibrational frequency to be able to interact with helpers in regions that are less vibrationally dense. This allows them to finish their journey. These helpers and guides also assist the individual to acclimate and adapt to living in their new dimension of reality. Conscious retrievals can be achieved by someone who is still in the physical realm through meditation/visualization techniques, OBEs, Shamanic Journeying, or lucid dreams.

SHARED DEATH EXPERIENCE

There's a growing number of accounts of living people who are having the experience of accompanying the dying person on part of their journey after death. This is most often reported by people who have close ties to the individual. More rarely, it can also happen to those who are taking care of the individual. The *Shared Crossing Project* is actively documenting accounts and reports of the shared death experiences, and they have observed that these experiences don't always occur precisely at the moment of death.

This was the case with my father, who passed, and my shared death experience with him that took place several days afterwards. This phenomenon can occur both at the bedside and remotely.

HOW TO HAVE A GOOD LIFE AFTER YOU'RE DEAD

Philosophy and Science Struggle to Understand Consciousness

During Covid, I read a book that took me through the history of philosophy from ancient times up to the present. Some of Plato's writings have stood up over time, but most philosophies have short tenures and are often influenced by the prevailing Zeitgeist of the era. As one died out, another took its place. For the past three hundred years, since the beginning of the *Age of Reason* there's been a merger of sorts between science and philosophy. The prevailing philosophies mostly lean towards the materialist's view of how our reality is constructed and functions.

We do have some push back on the mechanistic understanding of a universe made of physical stuff that evolved from pure chance. Present-day philosophers like David Chalmers ask for a paradigm shift in science and for it to consider that the entirety of reality is an intelligent conscious entity. Panpsychism and Biocentrism, for example, present the position that consciousness is the fundamental force driving our reality. Figures like Chalmers and theoretical scientists such as Robert Lanza are part of a growing contingent of thought leaders advocating for a reevaluation of how we perceive the fundamental nature of reality. They are aided by technological resources like *YouTube*, where their interviews and lectures are readily accessible. Widespread acceptance of their ideas may still be a generation away, however. Materialism remains the dominant philosophy even into this century. Science is not any closer to relinquishing the premise that matter is the fundamental substance of all reality and that mental states are derivative of interactions of material things. Its days are numbered, I suspect. The evidence against the materialist theory is mounting.

All philosophies are incomplete and fail to adequately address the complexity of the reality that we reside in, nor do we possess the mental equipment or necessary language to explore them adequately. We lack the vocabulary for describing the invisible worlds that reside outside of our physical senses. I have no issue with trying, because it's a positive thing that such ideas are always being wondered about. An open, curious approach is always welcome. The problem with the materialist view as a general philosophy is that it requires fealty to its dogma. There is no room for anything else to possibly be true. This creates a stasis and an impediment to ongoing inquiry.

I believe that our evolution as humans, society, and science depends on looking outside of the status quo. This requires us to perpetually consider the bigger picture and remain curious instead of being entrenched in a system of academic fiefdoms composed of folks trying to justify their university tenures. Let's urge science and humanity to abandon its comfort zones. More importantly, let's make it acceptable and not career-ending for the professional class to admit that they are wrong. It is not working as an explanation any longer and relies on magical thinking for its existence. It has become the very pseudo-science it criticizes.

We can start by widely accepting the core principle that our minds have limitations, as is the perceptual apparatus we use to place our ideas into a usable form, our brain. There are probably some smart fish who are explaining to other fish about the ocean and that there's this thing called land, but they are fish, with fish perspectives and must stay in the water. What they know about land can only be described within the context of their fish life. They only have fish language to explain it. Most have never seen land, so it is hard for them to conceive of, much less believe that there is such a thing as "land". Even if a theoretical "school" of thought arises, they can only go so far, and must mythologize about what land is. Just like humans trying to understand the reality we swim in, their assumptions are going to be incomplete. Such is the fate of human beings and their philosophical pursuits. What do you possess with an incomplete philosophy? In truth, not much.

It's always been my opinion that the best way for writers to approach their subjects is to keep it as accessible to as many people as possible. I know my audience will vary as to how familiar they will be with the information presented here. I search for a way to explain my thoughts so that it might accommodate those unfamiliar with these ideas. In researching my first book, I spent hundreds of hours watching videos on quantum mechanics, cosmology, philosophy, and neuroscience. I was struck by how little science understands the most fundamental underlying aspects of our universe. I learned that 97% of the universe is made up of things that physicists and cosmologists have never seen. Dark matter and dark energy are theoretical concepts and yet are widely accepted as fact. Little is understood about the concept of time or if the linear unfolding of time exists outside of our own perception. The most widely adopted notions of consciousness and our species' ability to perceive and maintain awareness of the world outside of ourselves, according to neuroscience, is solely a creation of the brain.

I will get right to the point: one of the things I know for sure is that our space-time universe and all the matter in it is derived from consciousness, not the other way around. I don't consider this statement dogmatic or even bold; it's ridiculously obvious when you evaluate the overwhelming evidence supporting it. At present, most scientists cannot make this assertion, although I suspect many would like to come out of their confined academic closets, so to speak, and let their freak flags fly. They are constrained by ideologies that sometimes mimic the strength of conviction seen in religious beliefs. Materialism is an unverifiable philosophy and, like other philosophies throughout human history, it too will eventually fall to the same fate.

Medicine has yet to recognize the existence of anything

surviving death because it can't admit this and stay true to its own orthodoxy. There can't be anything that survives death, because we are only our biology. Within the establishment medical community, consciousness is an epiphenomenon produced by chemical and electrical interactions within the brain. We are merely complex machines. These false narratives are a great impediment to knowledge. We could use that knowledge right now. We need to understand that we are infinite beings connected to our fellow humans, our planet, and the universe. Cardiologists are required to listen to the stories of their patients who have survived a heart attack and then describe their own resuscitation while floating above the proceedings. Millions of people are reporting these events, and, though they fly in the face of medical science's default understanding of the world, doctors on the front lines treating these cases are finding it harder to dismiss near-death experiences as hallucinations produced by a dying brain. We know from neuroscience that the brain seeks to conserve resources by default. That it would suddenly break with this biological habit and create elaborate reveries with novel content as the brain shuts down defies logic.

Science looks at phenomena such as telepathy, out-of-body, and near-death experiences and dismisses them as nonsense. The default reasoning is that there is no science-based evidence to support it. An elementary school child could penetrate the irony behind this conclusion, however. It hides behind an archaic scientific method that uses protocols designed for an 18th century world when the science of physics thought the universe was predictable and made only of interacting objects. Granted, these methodologies can work reliably for terrestrial experiments and the laws that govern physical objects. I am certainly not anti-science. Our technological advancements are astounding. Science has accomplished much, and we should celebrate the discoveries it has made. It fails to recognize the role of consciousness because it is stuck in an old paradigm of only considering objective reality in as much as it can be measured, reproduced, and falsified. Consciousness operates in a subjective reality and therefore must be tested differently.

It doesn't even accommodate the changes in understanding that have been around for a hundred years. In the early twentieth century we learned that our reality is strange and doesn't work at all the way that Newton understood it. Quantum Mechanics opened the door to a new way to understand the world. Instead of a universe of objects, they discovered that it is made of waves of probability. We are far removed from Newton's mechanistic understanding of reality. This died over a hundred years ago with the *Copenhagen Interpretation* and experiments such as the double slit experiment where we learned that matter is in an undetermined state until observed. The father of quantum science, Erwin Schrödinger admitted this when he wrote, *"Consciousness cannot be accounted for in physical terms. Consciousness is fundamental."*

HOW TO HAVE A GOOD LIFE AFTER YOU'RE DEAD

We now understand that matter exists simultaneously as both a wave and a particle. Its final state is reconciled only when it is measured. A measurement constitutes a type of observation, and experiments have repeatedly verified that matter doesn't coalesce itself until it's noticed by something. Simply having the intention to observe can influence the state and cause it to shift from a wave to a particle. It suggests that consciousness plays a fundamental role in shaping what we perceive as physical reality.

Each step has been taking us towards the realization that our universe is not actually physical. British Physicist James Jeans wrote this passage in his book, *The Mysterious Universe*:

The universe is beginning to look more like a great thought than a great machine. Mind no longer appears to be an accidental intruder into the realm of matter. We ought to hail it as the creator and governor of the realm of matter.

HIGH STRANGENESS

Research of psychical phenomena is ongoing all around the world in private foundations, university research facilities, and government-funded agencies. Both the public and private sectors provide funding for these types of projects at highly accredited institutions around the world. Money being granted for these projects is an implicit form of acknowledgement in my opinion. Funding flowing into these programs and the research continuing to expand tells us something. For example, the *University of Virginia*

Medical School's Division of Perceptual Studies (DOPS) has been investigating reincarnation, telepathy, OBEs, and the NDE phenomenon for over sixty years. The program has gathered thousands of cases, each of which has undergone rigorous scrutiny using scientific approaches that are adapted for these kinds of phenomena. The professionals working in *DOPS* are medical and science-based researchers. After sixty years, none of them has concluded that there is nothing more to explore.

We also should recognize the significant contributions around experiments on the non-locality of consciousness, which is not limited to the brain, explored by British biologist Rupert Sheldrake. His findings, conducted under rigorous protocols and published in journals, recognize the presence of telepathic communication in both mammals and humans. His theory on Morphic Fields and the presence of a collective sense of connection with others is captivating, and yet largely dismissed by the scientific community. They can't prove it doesn't exist; they just know it can't. Such is the life of a scientist who goes off the reservation.

Then there's the psychic spy program used by the Pentagon's Defense Intelligence Agency (DIA) for over twenty years, beginning in the 1970s and continuing until its end in 1996. The truth surrounding the program has been confirmed by journalists through publications made available by the Freedom of Information Act. The military believed in the program's success to the extent that it persisted as an intelligence-gathering method for two decades, securing annual approval for funding from Congress.

The methodology involved the use of the human mind to travel outside of time and space and bring back information that might protect our country. It was called "remote viewing". The building it operated out of was located on a military base in Fort Mead, Maryland. The strict double-blind protocols in place were rigorously maintained. An intelligence officer entered a relaxed altered state combined with a visualization process. The subject then set an intention to extend their awareness toward target coordinates contained in an envelope. These coordinates were unknown to the viewer or the operator in charge of that session. The primary mission of this program for much of its existence was to surveil circumstances on the ground inside of Soviet facilities and military bases using only the mind. What they were looking for was Soviet weapons development.

One of the intelligence successes coming out of these sessions was the identification of a Soviet super-submarine program that other intelligence sources failed to discover. This military's "psychic spy" program was publicly outed by a well-known journalist at the time, and this was the beginning of the end of the remote viewing program used by intelligence agencies. Embarrassed by the media coverage, the CIA commissioned a report designed to cast doubt on the program's effectiveness. The report stated that it only returned usable intelligence about a third of the time.

I met Joe McMoneagle, the most accurate remote viewer in the program, when I attended classes at the Monroe Institute. In our conversations, and later in his books, Joe addressed the CIA report and refuted many of the misrepresentations it contained. He said that not only was it a viable intelligence program with higher hit rates than stated. He also took issue with many of the characterizations of its relevancy as an intelligence-gathering tool.

Former President Jimmy Carter once acknowledged in an interview that remote viewing played a pivotal role in recovering an aircraft carrying crucial technology in Africa after all other search efforts had failed. The individual involved in its recovery provided precise longitude and latitude coordinates. This led to the plane's location via satellite and its subsequent retrieval. There are many stories like this available in the books written by Joe McMoneagle and other military personnel who participated in the program. As remarkable as these accounts are, I think the most important point is not its degree of effectiveness, but that it was effective at all. The very existence and longevity of the program can be considered verification, by a government agency no less, that consciousness is not solely localized to the brain.

As someone who is no stranger to high strangeness in a variety of forms, I can certainly respect the dilemma that faces someone who hears about traveling out of the body, claims of meeting dead relatives after a cardiac arrest, or reports of dreams that come true. There are terrestrial explanations for these things.

HOW TO HAVE A GOOD LIFE AFTER YOU'RE DEAD

Coincidences can happen. It's been shown that people may feel as if they left their body when a part of the brain is electrically stimulated, for example. A magician can sometimes duplicate a psychic's abilities. The fact remains, however, that correlation is not necessarily the same as causation. We can't discard findings on the basis that they can be replicated by other means.

Psychical phenomena fit nicely into the science of quantum physics, where reality is not fixed; rather, it comprises a collection of probability fields and energies that our senses can't detect. We live in the illusion of a reality that only actually comes into being when something observes it. That could be considered weirder than anything I'm proposing.

The universe operates through possibilities and indeterminate outcomes. Let's consider the scientific principle behind a well-established, repeatable experiment in physics known as "quantum entanglement". It states that when you take two distinct particles that interact with each other, they become permanently entangled to the extent that if one spins in one direction, the other will spin in the opposite direction at the same exact instant, regardless of the distance between them. On some level these entities are conscious of each other. Matter carries within it something that can remotely recognize itself. For the universe to exist, there must be an observer, and I propose that consciousness itself fulfills that role.

MIKE MARABLE

It pervades everything we know and can conceive of. We exist within it and it continually seeks avenues to manifest, understand itself and evolve.

Living With a Foot In Both Worlds

There are many of levels of knowledge and we are hard-wired with the desire to know and understand our natures. We adopt a curiosity about the history of the planet, the universe, and our place in it. At some point, we may question our purpose, what it all means, and whether there is life after death. The degree that we choose to delve into these questions is individual. You may be a person who is thinking about this. I suspect so, or you probably wouldn't be reading this book.

We are multidimensional, timeless beings who have taken on a corporeal form for the purpose of learning through the human experience. This learning progresses through every possibility of existence here on Earth, on other planets, and in other dimensions.

As we adapt to this experience in the human, there are some common themes we all share. The "Hero's Journey" for example, imparts lessons about courage and self-discovery, as well as love and service. It is the most common human storyline, and we all participate in it to varying degrees. We answer the call to adventure when we accept an incarnation opportunity.

As our story unfolds, we choose to share this reality system with others who are participating through the many stages of their own individual evolutionary path. We have one thing in common, and that is we are all visitors here. Sometimes we may feel like strangers in a strange land. It can be confusing to navigate. It's easy get off course from our original intention and see others as impediments to our plans. Though we appear to be similar in many respects, we maintain individualized programs within our physical containers. Our DNA holds the individual code for our unique mission.

We selected circumstances, skills and an egoic self that provides us with opportunities for a range of experiences. We are somewhat buffered from our true essence, and it can be difficult to remember who we really are and why we came here. We can be oblivious to the fact that we are all connected and are learning from each other on a subtle level below the threshold of awareness. Knowing this fact could be helpful because it might prompt us to be more tolerant and compassionate of others. That it remains cloaked is one of the conditions of this learning environment. It is a universal principal that we figure this out on our own and then make a choice as to what to do with this knowledge when we get it. It is quite perfect when you think about it.

HOW TO HAVE A GOOD LIFE AFTER YOU'RE DEAD

There are those in this learning environment who seem to think they can fast-track through the human experience. They may adopt spiritual practices such as meditation, choose a philosophy, or delve into books and workshops to hasten their evolution. Although it does demonstrate an intention and willingness to evolve—and this is certainly an important step—it is just a piece of the equation. It's simpler than many might imagine, though it's not easy to obtain. Our incarnational success depends more on a genuine depth of emotion and a profound desire in the realms of service, empathy, compassion, and love: particularly the kind of love where one unites with the energy of all life on this planet and embodies a commitment to be of service to it--to dissolve into it and give up one's life if necessary if it might benefit others.

Becoming a parent is a practice for this. Our pets can also serve as teachers about love.

I live with a foot in both worlds, as do you, though you may not be aware of it. I do not possess any special abilities; there are many who have profound experiences. We don't come here without the skills to complete what we came to do. We all have these, but many of us have forgotten how to use them. Indigenous cultures strive to preserve the esoteric teachings and transmit them from one generation to the next. In Western society, we have divested ourselves of this knowledge and often live in unnatural ways. Individually we have choices; it doesn't have to be this way. We can regain our identity. It starts with a choice and by asking big questions that open doors in the answering.

Modern humans may have forgotten the skill for traveling between worlds consciously, yet these abilities are present, ready to be activated. The flight instructions are in the program you walk around with every day in the cells of your body, your DNA. You venture out every night while your body sleeps, looking for opportunities to help yourself and your tribe. Try to remember.

I have an extraordinary, yet normal life in here in Southern California as a retired business owner. Most of my career was spent selling medical products and software technology. I have a wonderful partner of almost twenty years, and we enjoy each other's company very much. I am very fortunate to have her support and love. I don't subscribe to any ideology, philosophy, religion, or spiritual beliefs that might overly influence my objectivity. In 2016, I established an environmental nonprofit organization. I also serve as a climate leader for the international climate organization *Climate Reality Project*. I see myself as a global citizen and try to live that way.

Before I tell you how all this started, let me clear up a few things in advance about the motivations for the writing of this book. I don't relish the idea of being a public figure or to be seen as an authority on this or any other topic. I don't monetize off my experiences, offer classes, or otherwise promote myself as a teacher. I will answer questions and that is about it. I don't

HOW TO HAVE A GOOD LIFE AFTER YOU'RE DEAD

entertain requests to visit people in an OBE, dead or not. This would be an infraction upon their privacy and free will. Most of the proceeds from this book will go to animal sanctuaries.

I do enjoy writing, and this is my second book. I have another coming shortly after this one titled *The Wild Ride*. In that book I will go into adventures I have had traveling around in other timelines and alternative realities. It is as "wild" as it sounds.

Those of us who have interesting lives and stories to tell can help others by sharing our experiences along with what we have learned. I am also aware that these are my experiences and may not conform to the reader's understanding of reality. I do not see myself as any kind of ultimate authority. I present my informed opinions.

There are limits as to how far I will be able to bring you into my world much like when you return from a vacation, and you have difficulties conveying the experience so that it is made tangible for the people you speak to about your trip. I can only tell you about my journeys and possibly it will intrigue you enough so that you will venture out there yourself. Much of this may sound foreign to you, possibly strange. I understand how this can be the case. I never try to convince people. Glenda gave an answer to Dorothy at the end of the *Wizard Of OZ* when she asked why Glenda didn't tell her that she could have returned home at any time on her own: "Because you wouldn't have believed me my dear. You needed to find out on your own". We need to figure out this human experience for ourselves. This is our adventure to have. Mistakes are inevitable and part of how we learn. Advice is welcome, but I would never let someone else's version of reality have an oversized influence on how I live my life. I remain convinced that whatever transpires has some value contained in it if I am willing to pay attention to the message that is offered. There is no default program or template for living one's life that I can determine. If you turn left instead of right on a road, there is something to be discovered in that direction too. We might judge one to be better, but we can't really know. We seek the comfort of the familiar and yet we feel most alive when there is no certainty.

HOW TO HAVE A GOOD LIFE AFTER YOU'RE DEAD

ORIGIN STORY - HOW IT ALL STARTED

On a warm August day in 1987 my life changed dramatically, and it happened in moments. I am not talking about an accident or some unfortunate encounter with fate that we often associate with someone's whole world suddenly being turned upside down. In this case, it's as if it was altered from the inside out. The comfortable, familiar reality I knew suddenly shifted, and it would never entirely go back to the way it was before. I now see this as a positive event, but for a while, it interrupted my life. I came to understand experientially about who or what I am, and it is something far more expansive and interesting than I could have imagined. Encountering a deeper self and momentarily setting aside the persona of Mike Marable allowed me to perceive the persistent and convincing facade that dominates our perceptions of the Earth experience. Casting aside this illusion was a sobering and life-altering moment. It shakes things up. It does reassemble, but not in the same way as before.

Now, people may think this sounds wonderful, and it was initially. In retrospect, I can't say for sure that it was better to have this exact experience, but it does offer the benefit of being more aware of the restrictions and impediments that are an inherent part of the human experience. It allows for not becoming overly attached to the hindrances associated with the idea of being the person I believe I am. It's at least, if only momentarily, having an opportunity to perceive the world quite differently from my "normal" conscious state. I got a brief immersion into the knowledge of what a beautifully constructed set design there is behind the reality system we call the Earth.

I was dumbfounded for a long time as to why this happened to me. I am not a spiritual person. There were no years of struggles and searching for answers. I was not on any spiritual quest or dedicated to contemplation. I had no meditative practice; I am not sure I even knew what meditation was. I didn't undergo the harrowing ordeal of a near-death experience. Instead, it was a completely ordinary day in the midst of a relatively uneventful, trauma-free, contented life of an average 37-year-old man. I was struck by a metaphysical lightning bolt, and that's when the journey commenced. I refer to it as "The Wild Ride," my hero's journey. Once it started, I wholeheartedly accepted the invitation. I said yes to my "call to adventure." My curious nature kicked in and off I went.

It began when I stopped at a *7-Eleven* convenience store to pick up a cup of coffee in Richmond, Virginia, where I lived at the time. I was employed by a national company to sell medical products to nursing homes. It was like any other day. I was out making sales calls on existing customers. I will never know what would have happened in my life if I had skipped coffee that day. Would I have missed my cosmic rendezvous?

HOW TO HAVE A GOOD LIFE AFTER YOU'RE DEAD

I noticed when I walked out of the *7-Eleven* that there was a bookstore two doors down. I took my coffee into the store to see if they had any magazines I could buy to read at lunch. When I walked into the store, the sweet smell of incense was in the air and soft music was playing in the background. I asked the clerk if they had any sports magazines, and she said they didn't carry those kinds of publications. I decided to look around. I was an English literature major in college and love to peruse bookstores. Odd as it sounds though, I hadn't read very many books since college. Improvement of my mind was not high on my list of life priorities. I would describe myself at that time as a self-absorbed, moderately hedonistic man consumed more with climbing the ladder of monetary success. I had little interest self-awareness. It was the 1980s, and we were told greed was good. Though I wasn't "greedy" per se, I can look back now and see that my self-esteem was certainly tied up in how I presented to others. I was fully engaged establishing my place in the world.

Walking by a table, I noticed a book titled *Cosmic Revelation*, and I picked it up. It was written by someone named Ann Valentin. The title and cover piqued my curiosity, so I bought it just to have something to read at lunch.

I made some more customer stops and decided to go to a mall food court to eat. I remember every detail of that day clearly. I chose a Chinese dish with noodles, cabbage, and shrimp. Sitting down at a table, I pulled out the chopsticks, opened the book, and started reading the introduction. The book begins through an introduction by explaining that Earth is getting ready to enter an important time in its history—a coming shift or change in frequency that will alter its place in the solar system and the universe. It was not a topic that would normally have interested me or was even consistent with my understanding of the world, but I read on. Then something strange began to happen to me. I started to get warm, and I felt a buzzing sensation. The book went on to describe that there were people born into this time on Earth for the express purpose of "assisting in the transition." It said that these people had come to help raise the frequency of the planet and that this was needed to bring in and anchor "energies." These actions would help facilitate important conditions for the changes that would take place. It mentioned a term for these people. It called them "light workers," and it said that the person reading this book might just be such a person if they had received this book. I didn't know what any of this meant intellectually, yet some part of me did. Something was activated.

My next recollections are a bit hazy as it was at this point that the remembering started. The sensations picked up in intensity until I was aware of who I truly was beyond the personality I presented to the world. I understood why I had come here and its importance as a means for assisting the evolution of humanity. This lasted just a few minutes, and then my personality began to reconstitute itself. I looked around me, and the world was shimmering. I could see the energy fields of the people moving about. I felt a connection to them and to everything. My body and everything around me seemed to be vibrating. There was a rushing sound in my ears. I was not physically warm, but I felt a warmth radiating from inside me. Finally, I walked out of the mall to my car. I was feeling more alive than I had ever felt before. Excitement and bliss filled me, and I felt as if enthusiasm radiated from me—so much so that when I made my visit for an appointment at a local nursing home, the residents all seemed to lift their heads and look at me as I walked by. I must have been putting out a tangible energy because it was not a normal reaction. I felt it and, apparently, so did they.

In the days, weeks, and months that followed, I tried to make sense of what had happened to me. I didn't do drugs. No life-changing events had occurred that might have precipitated it. It had been calm waters, as far as I could remember, leading up to that day. I now was not the same person I had been before I "woke up" that day. My mind was ablaze with what I can only describe as something akin to downloading files into the computer of my mind. I was pulsing with energy, vibrating both day and night. I felt physically hot as if I was on fire from the inside. I still remembered the revelation about who I was, my mission, and what the human experience was about, but it started to feel unreal. I was losing that immediate knowledge, like a dream, as it started to fade. I was so excited that I now had this information, and I couldn't wait to share it. People were going to be so happy that they didn't have to worry, I thought. Like someone who had learned how all the magic tricks worked, I couldn't wait to tell people. What a relief to have all the answers, and who knew they were so damn simple! How could I not have known? It was so obvious. Other people would be as happy as I was when they too found out.

Over time, things settled down a bit, and I was able to step away and try to make sense of it all. I looked for context: why me and why now? I couldn't be the only person who was having this experience. Where do I begin to look? I went back to the bookstore; I thought maybe they might know where to start. The salesperson started talking about auras, energetic bodies, and past lives. It didn't seem to be relevant to what I was going through.

Meanwhile, every night when I went to bed, the light show would start. It began to concern me because it was growing more intense. I was not able to sleep because of the pulses of energy that were running through me. It was as if someone had hooked me up to a firehose of energy. I would find my arms and legs moving independently of my will. Then, I started to have out-of-body experiences almost every night. Sometimes, I would feel as if someone was pulling me out of my body and the sheets were being pulled off me. I heard people talking and sounds of closing doors or walking. I heard unfamiliar music and what seemed like the rushing of wind, like when you stuck your head out of a speeding car.

HOW TO HAVE A GOOD LIFE AFTER YOU'RE DEAD

During the day, I could still feel this vibration all around, and I felt a pressure in my head area as if someone was pushing hard on my forehead. Time and time again, I went back to the bookstore I had visited, trying to see if there was anyone who had heard of the kinds of things that were happening to me. Finally, someone suggested that I visit the *Edgar Cayce Foundation* in Virginia Beach. I decided to try this, since the beach area was in my sales territory. Again, not knowing where to start, I went into a bookstore located on the campus of *Atlantic University* that was part of the *Association for Research and Enlightenment*. After attending an afternoon introduction presentation on the life of Edgar Cayce, whom I had vaguely heard of, I searched the bookstore racks for titles that appeared relevant, and I bought several. I continued going to the *Edgar Cayce Foundation* for the next six months, and I attended many of their afternoon educational sessions. I got to know people there, and one of them suggested that I talk to a local psychologist because it sounded as if my experience was a little like something he had knowledge about.

I made an appointment with Gregory Scott Sparrow, Ph.D. He was in general practice as a psychologist and had some affiliation with the *Association for Research and Enlightenment*. We sat down and he listened patiently to my story and symptoms. He asked me how I felt about these experiences. I explained that although it was uncomfortable at times, I wasn't concerned that it was negative in any way. I felt positive and resourceful despite not getting much sleep at night. I felt curious more than anything else and assumed I wasn't losing my mind or was physically in danger.

There was no panic or anxiety around my experiences, which, in retrospect, seems a little odd. Why was I so confident that this wasn't pathological? I just wanted to understand what this was, why it happened, and wondered if it would ever lessen or stop. Most importantly, I wanted to know what to do with it. I felt that it was something important, but I had no idea where it was going to lead.

It was in this meeting with Scott Sparrow that I first heard of the Kundalini experience. The word sounded ominous to me, and I was a bit turned off. If I had gone to any other mental health professional, they would most likely have looked for some organic condition, such as frontal lobe epilepsy or a brain tumor. I doubt that their diagnosis would have included a coiled energy at the base of the spine that awakens in the initiates when they are ready for the path toward higher awareness. He said that he suspected that I had opened myself to this rare phenomenon. He told me that my symptoms were in alignment with a Kundalini opening because I did not seem to have any of the psychological conditions that might present for a psychotic break or mental instability. I asked why he thought this might be the case. He explained that he had gone through it himself, so he felt confident in his diagnosis. I asked him how long it would last. He said that he didn't have an answer for me, but he explained something along the lines that it takes as long as it needs to. It could even be years. I remember walking out of his office thinking there was no way I could take years of this.

In the days, months, and years following my event and the onset of those strange but fascinating symptoms, I have embarked on a lifelong quest not only to understand Kundalini, but to try to get some understanding about why it would happen to someone like me. I came to some conclusions after reading of similar experiences that precipitate what Anthropology Professor Joseph Campbell calls the "Hero's Journey." I had passed through the first stage, which Campbell calls the "Call to Adventure." It is in this stage that extraordinary events and circumstances often force a person out of the comfort of routine life to embark on a journey whose purpose includes a search for, and a return with, information that would benefit the village or tribe. There would be both challenges and allies to aid along the way, and there was no certainty that the hero would survive. It seems I had accepted the quest, probably even before I came into this lifetime. I was not without resources. I had a good foundation of knowledge from the original downloads received in the weeks and months following the opening, yet I needed verification that these things were true. I have now spent the past thirty-plus years chasing down answers. This has also served the purpose of gathering information for the village. This book is part of completing my task.

It has been both enlightening and sometimes a fool's errand. I have come to know that at this level of my being (operator of primitive wet equipment and linguistic limitations), I am never going to get to the bottom of it. This understanding has evolved over the many years and has become a relief of sorts. We all have our unique plan, and for some, remembering is essential. For others, it would be an impediment. The amnesia surrounding our true nature is not a bug. It's a dominant feature of this reality system we call being human, the human experience. We get the information we need to complete our individual missions, whatever they might be. There is never a small purpose in these missions, and time is irrelevant. A baby born in poverty who dies within days can learn as much or more than in a full-term lifetime. We don't understand something like this because, frankly, we can't from this vantage point. So, relax and enjoy the experience if you like; but, if you are inclined to read a book like this, I suspect you are not content with being a passive participant.

OBEs and Portals to Other Dimensions

Out-of-body experiences are a real phenomenon. Back when I first started having OBEs, long before the Internet, I had difficulty finding much information about it. Nowadays, there are many resources, including groups on social media--groups dedicated to research on the subject and experience stories. Amazon probably has a hundred books on related topics. *YouTube* has many videos and tutorials on how to achieve an out-of-body experience and astral travel. There's a variety of instructors offering classes and workshops both online and at retreats where participants can relax in the company of other seekers and try to attain this state. I wouldn't say it has reached mainstream in acceptance, but at this point, most have at least heard of it. Both *Netflix* and *Amazon Prime* regularly run fictional films that include story lines about altered states like out-of-body experiences. It is usually addressed in a sensationalized and spooky way. Two of the more recent ones that come to mind are, *OA* and *Behind Her Eyes*. I really liked *OA*.

This section is provided to serve to briefly familiarize the reader with this natural phenomenon that anyone can, and does, participate in, though they may not recognize and remember its taking place.

MIKE MARABLE

After my experience in 1987 and the onset of nightly out-of-body experiences, I recalled reading a book back in my college days about a guy who lived not far from where I grew up in Virginia. His OBEs came on abruptly, and he thought he might have a brain tumor or worse; maybe he was dying or losing his mind. Robert Monroe was a courageous man who found a treasure within his own being. Hidden there like a golden Easter egg was the ability to go to the worlds that people enter when they die. Just as with Emmanuel Swedenborg centuries before, what he found often surprised him. I met Robert during my visits to the Monroe Institute, the consciousness research facility that he established in the Blue Ridge mountains of Virginia. I found him to be funny, self-deprecating, and generous. He knew a lot and had seen some things, yet he never once came across as any kind of seer, nor did he take on the role of the all-knowing sage. If you asked him a question, he was just as likely to smile with a gleam in his eye as if to say, "I can't tell you that. You need to find out on your own." I was fortunate that I had his experiences as a reference when mine started happening.

Results from public surveys conducted over the years indicate that around ten percent of the population claims to have had a conscious out-of-body experience during their lifetime. That's a lot of people when you think about it. Some of these OBEs overlap with the phenomenon known as the near-death experience. Advancements in patient resuscitation techniques have resulted in more people being revived following cardiac events where the heart and brain activity stop functioning, yet the person can see from above what is being said and done to revive them. The accuracy and detail in the recollections of so many people diagnosed as clinically dead can't be explained away. Some thirty percent of these patients report experiencing the out-of-body phenomenon during these trauma events.

If one were to experience these states and go to a psychiatrist, they would categorize them as "dissociative states". The clinical description of such states includes terms like "hallucinations" and "delusions". In their materialist world view these would be pathological conditions to be treated with drugs. There are conditions that mimic these states that are actual mental health conditions: schizophrenia for example. These are characterized by confusion about what is and isn't part of the sense of self or real.

People who report OBEs have no problem separating what happens in these experiences from normal waking consciousness. Neuroscience makes no accommodation for these kinds of experiences. There is no non-local aspect of consciousness or self because it is produced by the brain. When someone has a dissociative event, it's assumed that it's because their brain is broken. Mental health practitioners wouldn't know what to do with high functioning types who could test as more psychologically healthy precisely because they have these kinds of experiences.

OBEs THROUGHOUT HISTORY

For thousands of years, religious and secular texts have described the phenomenon we think of as out-of-body experiences. For example, we can refer to writings going back to Ancient Egypt, specifically the *Egyptian Book of the Dead,* which makes references to the *KA,* an aspect of our consciousness that separates from the body and visits the underworlds. The Shamans of indigenous cultures around the world hold an important place in their society. They are important leaders within their communities and are celebrated for their skills, which bring great benefit and healing to others. They are tasked to venture into the realms of their ancestors for the purpose of returning with knowledge to be given to the people. They do this through disembodied consciousness that is free to explore the regions occupied after death and meet with the ancestors.

Tibetian Buddist philosophy has its own sacred texts that detail how to travel into the invisible worlds beyond the physical. These are considered to be one of the abilities or *Siddhis* that can present themselves through meditation and a devotion to seeking universal truths. The *Tibetan Book of the Dead* is one of the most resourced books in the history of the world for people seeking answers around what happens after we die. It provides detailed instructions on successfully navigating post-physical existence. The book includes ways to avoid getting lost in the illusions and dreams of *Bardo.* This would impede the progress of a soul's journey towards final enlightenment and freedom of the reincarnation cycle. People of the Christian faith will find references to out-of-body states in the Bible. For example, in *Ecclesiastes,* there is mention of leaving the physical body and being tethered by a "silver cord." Paul, following his spiritually transformational experience, wrote about the various heavens one can travel to.

In more recent times, the first credible accounts of traveling outside the body into other worlds came to us through the writings of 18th-century inventor, mathematician, biologist, philosopher, and scientist **Emmanuel Swedenborg** (1688-1772). Having grown up a devout Lutheran and the son of a clergyman, Swedenborg was a deeply religious man living at the height of the materialist *Age of Reason.* He had much to lose in telling his strange tales of traveling into lands occupied by the dead.

Following an ecstatic awakening, he wrote that he encountered a supreme being who touched his head, after which he began having a variety of mystical experiences. These included incidences of leaving his body and meeting with the departed in worlds that looked like the one he was living in. He chronicled this in exquisite detail in his book, *Heaven and Hell.* His experiences in the hereafter surprised him greatly. He expected the beatific heavens that his faith described. Instead, he found people living and conducting their afterlives much as they had been during their earthly existence. He often commented that he would meet people he had known in life and was shocked at their lack of progression. He found what many of us who travel find: that some people don't change much after they die. They often resume a life not unlike what they had left here on Earth.

Swedenborg's writings greatly impacted the romantic poets, particularly William Blake, and later the *Transcendentalist Movement's* writers, poets, and philosophers. Swedenborg influenced the works of Ralph Waldo Emerson, Henry David Thoreau, and Walt Whitman. Helen Keller was also a fan of Swedenborg's writings. There are still societies dedicated to studying his work even today. It's hard to imagine anyone, much less a famous person and scientist like Swedenborg, putting his life and reputation in such obvious peril. He was obviously a man in possession of a great integrity and courage.

There was a revival of interest in mysticism and the supernatural during the eighteenth, nineteenth, and early twentieth centuries. It prompted the rise of clandestine groups operating outside the prying eyes of academia. The movement towards materialist rationalism had grown and was now the dominant world view. Still the gravitational pull towards what is real never lets up and certain members of the intellectual class who had access to ancient manuscripts were intrigued with the notions that reality was far more complex than what science was offering up. They met secretly in groups discussing the classical texts and philosophers such as Plato.

HOW TO HAVE A GOOD LIFE AFTER YOU'RE DEAD

Within their meetings and discussions, they found an opening and the possibility of worlds that existed beyond this one. In addition to the work of Swedenborg, who was almost a contemporary, they referenced the writings of the ancient societies mentioned earlier. They also had access to the texts of *Christian Gnosticism*, the secret knowledge of the *Freemasons*, the *Brotherhood of the Rosy Cross*, and *Rosicrucianism*. Most notable of these groups regarding out-of-body experiences in the modern era was the *Theosophical Society*, a group made up primarily of scholars and intellectuals founded in New York in the latter half of the 19th century. The theosophists referred to the practice of traveling as *astral projection,* taken from the Greek and Latin root *astralis* or star. Out of this came the idea of realms existing up among the stars called the *astral planes.* This is where dreamers and others can visit while alive and go to live after death. Astral traveling is the conscious volition to leave the physical world during meditation or sleep and travel to the astral planes. These places contain inhabitable realities for those still living who wish to visit using the astral body and those who no longer possess a physical body after death.

Robert Monroe called them *belief system areas*; some of us use the term *consensus realities*. These places seem to be endless in variety. The higher their frequency, the less physical they appear.

Accounts of people living in earthlike realities after they have died continued to be of great interest in the 18th and 19th centuries. It got the attention of eminent American psychologist William James, who reported and wrote about his patients' experiences of traveling into other worlds. Austrian architect, journalist, and mystic Rudolf Steiner (1861-1925) wrote about his own visionary experiences and astral traveling in his seminal book *How to Know Higher Worlds* (1904). In 1965, in Minnesota, a nonsecular church calling itself *Eckankar* taught that the soul exists separate from the body and can travel to learn and be closer to God by learning dream and soul travel. It is commonly thought that Eckankar's founder, Paul Twitchell, was greatly influenced by the Eastern teachings on this subject. He practiced these disciplines before founding a group devoted to the spiritual practice of *soul traveling*. *Eckankar* currently has branches in 120 countries, according to their website.

For most of you reading this book, the most familiar name associated with the phenomenon of out-of-body experiences is **Robert Allan Monroe** (1915 -1995). He adopted the term "out of body experience" during his association with Russell Targ, who came up with the descriptive name. For Monroe, the term astral travel carried the baggage of mystical context from its previous use. He did not care to have his research associated with the occult.

Monroe, at the time of his first experience, was making a living as an executive in the radio broadcast industry. He became interested in the potential benefit of sleep learning and used sound recordings at night as he slept. He is now known for the *Hemi-Sync* technology that employs sound to induce altered states of consciousness. His first experience can possibly be attributed to a lucky accident, one that took a man from the world of technology and business on a lifelong adventure into the unknown. Fortunately, he provided humanity with a detailed account of what he saw and experienced. It changed his life in ways he probably could never have imagined for himself.

One afternoon in 1958, while living in Westchester, New York, he found himself floating above his body during a nap. The experiences continued to occur and, at first, he had little control over them. The full story can be found in his first book, *Journeys Out of The Body* (1971). Monroe went on to write a series of books about his adventures in other realities, and they are all still available in print. He founded the *Monroe Institute*, a not-for-profit research and education center dedicated to exploring the nature of consciousness. It was out of these programs that he and fellow "explorers" consciously induced OBEs using sound technology to alter their state of consciousness into a "mind awake, body asleep" condition. This proved conducive to achieving a separation and liftoff that allows for our consciousness to travel into other realities and other dimensions of time that are not readily available to our waking state mind.

These were scientifically minded people with little inclination toward the mystical. It is my understanding that their training was not unlike that of astronauts. They could be considered "aeronauts" of the mind, traveling in search of other realities. What they found were worlds as real for the inhabitants living there as this one is for us. These frequency bands exist beyond our waking perceptions. Most conveniently, our senses are specifically designed for this one. Can you imagine how hard it would be to live your life if other realities kept bleeding into this one? Our brains serve as a transducer and filter to make sure this doesn't happen. When we sleep or meditate, this equipment can go offline temporarily. If we are curious and diligent, we can learn to take advantage of this and explore.

Just as Swedenborg wrote hundreds of years prior, those explorers working out of the *Monroe Institute* found people living in other dimensions of reality. Some of these appeared more earthlike than others. These are the consensus realities that I and other explorers visit in our OBEs.

Jurgen Ziewe is a German-born graphic artist living a gentleman's life near the coast in Southwest England. He is also the most prolific and talented out-of-body explorer I have ever met. That he is not one of the more famous people in the world is beyond me. I consider him to be like a modern-day Swedenborg, given the breadth of his experiences. Jurgen is a traveler and explorer with skills that, in my opinion, place him in a lane that few can claim. The depth and detail of his recollection and writing on his journeys is accessible to the reader. He is, like Swedenborg, Monroe, and Steiner, a modern renaissance man who possesses both artistic and

HOW TO HAVE A GOOD LIFE AFTER YOU'RE DEAD

technical talent. As a writer, he approaches his experiences with scientific curiosity and intellectual rigor. His reporting has no ideological bent and is free of mystical trimming. He reminds me of a good journalist striving just to make sure that he gets the story right.

Jurgen's books and videos have reached many hundreds of thousands of people. I suspect that he will never know all the people he has helped to calm the anxiety that many have about the idea of death. I am honored that he agreed to contribute to this book. We also did some podcast conversations together, discussing our experiences. They can be found on his *YouTube* channel. I recommend that anyone who is interested in these topics spend some time watching his videos and reading his three books.

WHAT DOES IT FEEL LIKE?

Every person, and probably most animals, separate from their physical bodies at night during sleep. The phase shift is timed with what we think of as the REM cycle of sleep that occurs roughly every ninety minutes. People who have conscious awareness during these shifts and remember them are the ones reporting that they have out-of-body experiences. You have probably awakened during one of these and didn't realize that your consciousness had separated from your physical body because it doesn't feel any different.

Your physical body is the densest representation of the several body states that you inhabit. Your energy bodies are invisible to you and others, but they are no less real or consequential than the one you can see. When someone experiences a conscious OBE, they have shifted normal waking awareness into one of these other bodies that vibrate at a higher frequency. This is like a tuning fork that presents different tones based on the density of its construction. These bodies are not made of dense matter, so they are not subject to the rules governing the physical world. They exist in other dimensions. These dimensions do not have the same limitations nor are they governed by the rule sets of the physical system that we think of as the "real world."

The next densest energy body, which is a level immediately removed from your physical one in frequency, is the one that most people occupy when they first realize they have completely separated. It feels just like the physical body. It is an energetic duplicate, and it continues to interact with your physical body even though that body is lying in bed asleep. You may be standing beside your bed and feel the carpet beneath your feet while listening to yourself or your partner's breathing. When I look around, everything looks pretty much the same, yet not exactly so, because although it appears to be a duplicate of your physical space that overlaps the original, it has been impacted by your thoughts and others who may have lived there before you. For example, it may look pretty much the same except it is painted a different color because, in your imagination, you have thought about changing the color. Your thoughts impact your surroundings. Maybe this helps explain why it's so hard to test people's abilities. When we get out, we are in this similar dimension that overlaps the physical one, yet it can differ enough that a specific target is not accessible.

When someone is conscious during the exiting of the body, there can be a feeling of vibration, falling, being pulled out of the body, or a rushing sound as one wakes up in one's energy body. My experience, and that of others, is that these indicators dissipate over time. As one gets more accustomed to moving in and out, the clues become much more subtle.

A person has access to these skills and can begin to navigate various dimensions of reality. This is where intention becomes important. Decisions about where to go and what to do are important; otherwise the dominant state of mind will take a traveler to places they may not want to go. There are all kinds of places and, frankly, some of them can be unsavory. There is something for everyone in these realms. This surprises people who may think it only conforms to the accounts of those who have near-death experiences. Those accounts are accurate for the people who report them. Their consciousness has exited under unique circumstances, and something akin to a homing signal takes them to what I call a "landing area". These places can correspond to the desires and beliefs. My sense is that there is something different about the NDE from our actual final act of death. It is as if there is some measure of grace built into the near-death event. I have no proof that this is true, of course, because no one returns from the final death experience.

This is one of the differences from an OBE traveler's experience, although we can certainly visit those areas reported by someone who had an NDE if our frequency level is high enough. It's important to mention that we cannot cross into levels that resonate at a higher frequency than our base state of consciousness allows, just as an amateur violinist can't get an invitation to play at Carnegie Hall.

Our default frequency for this life is a bit like a cosmic passport. One of the ways to gain access to more frequencies is to cultivate a default energy for love of self and others. The more this becomes the prevailing energy you inhabit, the more it provides an opportunity for higher frequency experiences and the locations that open. We go as deep and far as our frequency can take us.

It can be difficult to hold onto the conscious OBE state, and it's easy to become distracted. Our emotions and intention can influence how long we can stay "out". I call being pulled back to the body "blinking out." When you get to the experiences section of the book, you will see that this happens. My go-to way of exiting my physical body is to "roll out" of bed in my second state. You literally roll out just like you would in the physical. Some people float out, but that has never worked for me. Sometimes, after I

HOW TO HAVE A GOOD LIFE AFTER YOU'RE DEAD

blink out, I have a false awakening. This means I may think I have woken up in my bed, but I haven't. I have returned to the state of being separated and in close alignment with my body, yet it feels as if I am fully awake. When this happens, I roll out again. These are all techniques I have learned over the many years of doing this. I recognize the subtle signs of when I have separated that many people miss. This is the reason I have a lot of OBE opportunities. My current rate is one to three times a week. I can hold state for long periods and have hours-long experiences because I use a supplement made from a flower that helps keep the executive functions, including memory, online. It doesn't produce an OBE nor is it even a catalyst. It allows your waking consciousness to have some level of alertness during the sleep cycle. It helps some remember the experience too. This is why you will see the level of detail in my experiences. I am essentially fully awake with my full consciousness while traveling. I write the experiences down immediately upon my return. It is no different as far as the quality of experience than going to the grocery store and coming back to report the details of your actions and encounters. It's that clear for me. The flower extract is a useful and safe cheat for remembering. I learned it from other people who use it this way for lucid dreaming. Noticing and remembering is key.

The first time you find yourself outside your body, it can be exhilarating. You suddenly know with complete certainty what you could only intellectually hope for before the experience: that you are more than your body. From there, it's not difficult to take it to the next logical conclusion. If you aren't just your body, then the potential for surviving death becomes a very real possibility. To know that you can't really die is liberating. There are plenty of things in the world to worry about, and this one is suddenly removed from the list.

What Do I Need to Know Before I Leave

The theme of this book focuses on helping people prepare for their own death and what might follow. Depending on your age and health, you may have more leeway in putting this off than others do. I suggest that it warrants some consideration, no matter what your status is. After all, it is arguably the second most important moment in our lives. Most people know very little about it, and fewer still engage in any preparation. Those of us who travel to the other side in OBEs and NDEs can offer some general guidance about what to expect. Everyone's experience will be unique to them, of course, but we know from hundreds of thousands of accounts logged by researchers over the last fifty years that there are some common elements.

The most important thing I would like all people to know is that the moment your heart stops, the last time you take a breath, you are as alive as you were the moment before that event.

You have the same personality and consciousness that you had in the life just lived, at least initially. Explorers like me who travel in the OBE state can go into the realms that people report in an NDE. These other realities are occupied by people who left the human experience. We interact with the inhabitants, and they share information with us. In my case, I have done this hundreds of times spanning over thirty years, and I can confirm that the receiving areas frequently reported on by those who arrive there in a NDE have some consistent features.

A person who has a cardiac arrest may be resuscitated after a few minutes, yet it can feel like hours. This phenomenon of time dilation may offer the person an opportunity to look around and learn things before returning. When I help people cross over, I ask them questions, observe the helpers after the handoff, and sometimes they share things with me. The information in this section was collected from a combination of sources over many years.

The first thing you might want to remember when you find yourself in one of these environments after you physically die is to make a quick peace with the fact that this lifetime is done. There is nothing you can do to change anything from the physical life just lived; no scores can be settled, and no amends can be made. It's good to get those behind you now.

There is no need to stick around after you are out of the physical body. The longer you linger, the more difficult it will be for you and your loved ones. If you ask for help to assist, there will be a guide to help at any time. If it is dark, look for any light you can find and go there. It is easier to see the helpers and guides around a light source, even if it looks like a candle that's a block away. They are there even if you can't see them. Try to clear the mind and raise your frequency with positive thoughts and emotions. It is a good Idea to set the intention in advance to have a guide waiting for you as you cross over. You can do this right now; there is no time as we know it outside of this physical environment. The person or group that meets you may be someone you are familiar with, but not always. It might be a family member, but sometimes not the one you expected.

You will find yourself in a body that may be indistinguishable from your physical body.

If you have doubts about whether you did in fact die, you can do a reality test by pushing your fingers into something or jumping up. If your fingers penetrate it or you float back down, you will know you died. Once you have your confirmation, you can begin looking for assistance. In most cases, there will be a light above or in front of you. It may resemble the sun or the moon if the environment is dark. Always move in the direction of the light source. Just the intention to get to the light will get you moving towards it. There may be more than one light source; you will be particularly attracted to one of them. After you go through the light, which is very pleasant, you may find yourself in a lovely setting. It uld be a field, mountains, gardens, parks, and even the ocean. There will be greeters and well-wishers. It's a reunion and celebration of your achievement. Every life is a success. Only the bravest venture into the human experience.

It is important to remember that what you believed in life and your expectations can have an influence on what you experience during this time. If you were deeply religious, you may see the symbols of that religion. This is so you aren't disoriented by what you find. This is particularly helpful to those who are under the impression that there is no afterlife.

Over time, you will be told by elders about the reality you will inhabit. This unfolds in a timetable that is comfortable for the new arrival. You can land in a location that conforms more to your expectations. If you have been sick or had a difficult life in the run-up to your physical departure, you may go into what looks like a hospital setting with doctors and nurses. Great care will be provided to help you recuperate and get your strength back. Some adapt quickly and move on to the next stage. If you decide you want to say goodbye or give a message to those that you left behind, including some notice of your arrival, you can be shown how to do this through dreams and intuition. Your strong bond and a will to do so, combined with the will of another person, can cooperate to make this happen.

After all, the only thing separating you from them is

HOW TO HAVE A GOOD LIFE AFTER YOU'RE DEAD

frequency; distance is not an obstacle.

You may experience a life review. During this process you will have a condensed multidimensional panoramic immersion into the life just lived from a perspective you can't imagine right now. This may sound daunting, yet it is an important part of the process. Though some who have an NDE report a life review, it usually takes place in your post-physical process when the person is ready to receive the information it contains. There is no judgement about anyone's life, though you may judge yourself. There are counselors to advise about why that isn't necessary or helpful.

Over time, your personality, and characteristics of the lifetime you just left will partially fade. It may begin to feel like the life you just left was like having a dream. You will begin to see the bigger picture and why it transpired as it did and probably have a good laugh about things that you fret over right now. Those you left in the physical who follow you may arrive in a place so you can greet them if you like. You can also leave a projection of yourself there for them that will contain love and acceptance no matter what difficulties you may have had in that life. There will be choices to be made; they are always your choices. They are not likely to be the ones you think you will make from your current perspective.

I hope this helps provide you with some assistance, both for yourself and those who cross over into that other dimension as they leave behind the spacesuit used for the adventure into the human.

Obviously, this is only a high-level overview of these experiences. To say that there are many variations and possibilities in these realities would be a gross understatement and this overview is only to serve as a guide attempting to provide the broadest possible canvas as to what I and others like me who travel have encountered. There are most likely a vast myriad of possibilities beyond our reach and much we can't know because there are frequencies of realities that are closed to us. That travelers and people who have NDEs find some similarities is important information to have I think, and so I have provided this summary of the most common and consistent scenarios that we encounter that it might provide some benefit to the reader. As always, a curious and open mind is beneficial. A map is not the actual territory.

HOW TO HAVE A GOOD LIFE AFTER YOU'RE DEAD

DYING EVERY DAY

The moment we take our first breath of consciousness and enter the human, the clock begins ticking on our time here. Linear time sequenced out into moments, days, and years is part of the earth's experience. Neuroscience has discovered that we carry around with us a sense of unfolding time, a mental and biological clock that is cognizant of a sequential passing of moments. This provides the illusion of a progressive forward movement from a past that no longer exists and a future that is yet to be. We can give ourselves mental instructions to wake up in the morning at a particular time, and the odds are good that we will hit it right around the intended target. My dog comes looking for his dinner or walk at specific hours during the day, not varying much more than fifteen minutes regardless of the time of year.

The physical body marks the passage of time, too. Our chromosomes have ribbon-like structures called telomeres that shorten over our lifetime in coordination with other systems, like our immune response, that make us more vulnerable to disease.

Most of us only begin to seriously contemplate death when the physical equipment starts to wear down. It could happen when a doctor tells us our time may be running out. Dying is part of living; it runs concurrently. The two processes cannot be separated; they are indivisible. The unassailable fact is that your time here is always running out. It could happen after you finish this sentence or fifty years from now. This is not a glitch or system failure in the universe. It is more like a fundamental necessity built into the evolutionary process in the unfolding and education surrounding whom you really are beyond the personality. It is the part of transformational component for living in the truest sense of what the word "living" means. Just as a caterpillar must die to its former self to become the butterfly, it is the catalyst for changes in all of nature. Die often and die well, or as the ancient Greek mystical practices of the Eleusinians explain it, "If you die before you die, when you die, you will not die". Embrace the continuation of your unfolding towards being even more magnificent than you can understand right now.

HOW TO HAVE A GOOD LIFE AFTER YOU'RE DEAD

YOU ARE NO STRANGER TO OTHER WORLDS

We have a dress rehearsal for the stage beyond our earth's lifetime every night: it is called dreaming. When you fall asleep, you transition out of normal waking consciousness and enter the world of the dead; it happens in your dreams.

There will be more detail on this in a later section. This reality is as real a state of consciousness as your daytime world. These daily death events and the dream world prepare us for the main event when we drop our spacesuit and inhabit these realms full-time. I remember that once I was on a Roman battlefield in a dream. I was fatally stabbed in the gut by a sword during a fierce battle. I felt it painlessly enter my body and fall to the ground. As I lay there bleeding out, I became conscious that it was a dream. Instead of panicking, my reaction was that this was a good opportunity to experience what it is like to die. As I lay there feeling the life force leave my body, I grew drowsy. I fought back the sleepiness because I wanted to cross over fully conscious. After what seemed like many minutes, I had the sensation of falling. A great calm then came over me as I accepted my death and waited for what was to come. I entered a light, and a great contentment took over. I was ecstatic; how wonderful it all seemed.

I awoke slowly, finding myself lying in my bed, a bit disappointed that I was back in this reality. I was given the gift of being able to complete a simulation of the transition via a lucid death and remain fully conscious. I had no doubt at that moment, and even now, that this is what it feels like to die from the physical body. I have had this kind of dream several times now, and it always follow a similar process. Dying in that reality delivers us here, and I believe dying in this reality delivers us to another one. I expect to wake up when that moment arrives, maybe even in a comfortable bed, and think about my human experience, "Wow! That was a wild dream".

Within the Hindu philosophy on how to have a conscious death, there are practices a person can master that are designed to help avoid falling into these unconscious dreams referred to as the *Bardo*, the dream-like worlds of illusion following physical death. It includes a state of forgetting and can delay a person's arrival into the higher worlds. Learning to lucid dream is one of the ways we can remain conscious of our physical death and maintain our awareness. This way, we may be able to walk to these realities fully conscious of our circumstances. This is called a "conscious death".

HOW TO HAVE A GOOD LIFE AFTER YOU'RE DEAD

DEATH MAKES A COMEBACK

For most of our history on this planet, generations thought about death a lot more than our current society does. We modern humans can try to put it out of our minds, manufacturing the illusion of immortality for ourselves. Previous generations lived with a more prescient relationship with the reality of death. We live in a time where life expectancy has increased to an average of almost eighty years, augmented by advancements in medical science and a better understanding of nutrition and health. Our ancestors lived under the specter of knowing that life is fragile--that at any moment the end could come calling. The chance of making it to thirty was no better than a fifty-fifty chance. A bad cut on the foot or even a cold that led to an infection could take a person out in short order.

In 1900, when government agencies began to keep mortality statistics in America, the average life expectancy was just 47. We know from the writings of the ancient Greeks and Egyptians that their entire lives focused on getting ready for death, embracing the understanding that our time on earth was a temporary layover and eternity played out somewhere else.

Those of us born in the latter half of the 20th Century have gotten a respite from having to think about it until we get closer to the end. Medical advancements have been able to extend lifespans to the point that many believe they may be able to cheat death by having their consciousness downloaded into a computer or freezing their bodies until a cure is found for whatever killed them. The medical community and pharmaceutical companies depict a disease like cancer as if it were a foe or monster to be dispatched instead of a natural function of cellular activity when the immune system can't contain the damage from aging or environmental toxins. We produce at least a thousand cancer cells every day our life. It's not something we suddenly catch; we live with it continuously. It is as natural to get an illness as it is to not have one. People get sick, and sometimes they die from their illness. We must not think of this as failure on our part because society has adopted this mindset. Instead, let's consider the quality of life over quantity of years. I think about what was accomplished by great artists, musicians, and inventors in relatively short lifespans by today's standards. Modern cultures are more likely to waste the added years looking at their phone screens.

  We can look to animals, who have a shorter life and see this play out in a contracted scenario. They get older, become sick and die. We don't look at them and say, "Gee, this could have been avoided if they just worked out more."

  I am reminded of the depiction of death as the chess opponent in Ingmar Bergman's film the *Seventh Seal*, an opponent to beat or outsmart. This kind of "can do" optimism is now sold so regularly to people in our society about almost everything that it's not hard to see why some apply it towards death too. We've reached a point where the very act of dying is treated like failure.

HOW TO HAVE A GOOD LIFE AFTER YOU'RE DEAD

If only we had taken more supplements and fought harder, we could have beaten this thing.

Death, as a common topic for discussions, has been shuttered in modern polite society. I'm not sure how long this taboo has been the case. You would think that an event so prevalent, one that every person on Earth shares in, would come up more often in conversation. If you want to clear a room, bring up this subject. I found out through experience that it's not considered an appropriate topic at a dinner party. When I tell people I am writing a book, they naturally ask what it's about. When I tell them death, they rarely ask a follow-up question.

I go back and forth in my thinking; is it that we are more frightened of it, or is it that we are just avoiding anticipating it because of the comforting illusion of immortality? Has it been pushed out so far, in some cases to over a hundred years, that death has lost its relevance to modern times? Life insurance companies have had to grapple with this conundrum as a business; that is, how to get people to think about their own future and take proactive measures in preparation for the inevitable. Social psychologists discovered that we cannot relate to our future selves any more than we can to a stranger.

The arrival of the pandemic in 2020 and the possibility that we may not be alive a week into the near future brought the reality home in an immediate way. For the first time in our generation, we could walk out of our home, go to the grocery store, and a week later be dead. We learned first-hand what past generations dealt with regularly in the times before vaccines. It tends to focus the mind. This is our generation's mass introduction to the concept of death, and it didn't go well. Some didn't take it seriously, or maybe it was denial combined with coping strategies that caused people to make decisions about their wellbeing that were not in their best interest. Personal decisions to not wear a mask in public may have been an act of defiance against authority. More likely, it was a veiled form of denial.

We are inclined to not be able to cognitively accommodate that our lives could end in such a manner when we are feeling robust and healthy in the moment.

History has demonstrated time and again that societal catastrophes on the scale of the event we lived through, where a significant number of our fellow humans have suffered and died, were inevitably followed by a cultural and economic renaissance. I could go so far as to say that these kinds of occasions are programmed into the human experience as an opportunity to reset old patterns and open us up to new vistas on our potentialities. Being faced with our own individual mortality can induce the same effect in our lives if we are open to it. To be reminded that this isn't going to go on forever and that our time here is finite can allow us the mental space to recognize what is important and create more urgency in pursuit of our callings. Being actively conscious that we

HOW TO HAVE A GOOD LIFE AFTER YOU'RE DEAD

will die has a way of focusing the mind. We should ponder it and can do so without relishing its arrival. After all, it is the second most important experience any of us will ever have. It behooves us to give it some thought.

MIKE MARABLE

Choosing A Good Death

There can be much to take care of after a person dies. Many of us have complex lives with lots of entanglements, both financial and personal. My mother died suddenly at the age of 63 in 1994. I am her only child, and other than an elderly grandmother and uncle, there was no one to help with handling her affairs after she passed.

I got a call from my uncle that she died in the hospital after a bout of pneumonia. I immediately flew down to San Antonio, Texas, from Virginia, entered her house, and started going through drawers and cabinets, trying to find everything I could regarding her insurance policies, a Will, real estate, bank accounts, and loans. Fortunately, she did have a Will, but I had to piece everything else together. I made the funeral arrangements and wrote her obituary. Like most people, she didn't plan to die. I didn't want my grandmother to have to deal with all this. After all, it wasn't just my mother who was gone, it was also her daughter.

HOW TO HAVE A GOOD LIFE AFTER YOU'RE DEAD

My dad was the complete opposite when it came to making prior arrangements for when his day came. He had everything taken care of in advance, right down to what food would be served and each musical number played at his Celebration of Life gathering. Before he transitioned the day after Christmas in 2013, he had made sure no detail would be left open for someone else to have to try to manage in his absence. He was eleven years older than my stepmother, and he wanted to make sure she wasn't left with having to take care of all the logistics of what would follow when he moved on. She and I were like guests at his event, and literally nothing had to be arranged by us. The speakers were already selected, the room and reception area decorated in the assisted living facility, and the space reserved for his ashes in the church grounds.

These are obviously two extremes; most of us would likely fall into the middle if we were to leave tomorrow. It made me much more cognizant of the importance of getting all these arrangements made in advance so that we don't have added stress in our final days. It can also serve as a practical farewell gift for the very people we care about. It is going to be hard for them, obviously, and it doesn't take much effort to remove this burden during a time that could be partitioned to all for their grieving. Then, there's our own peace of mind to consider, both before and after transition. An empty "unfinished business" bucket makes for an easier transition.

What constitutes a good death in modern terms is more

likely to defer to the medical community's definitions. These may include exhausting treatment options, and once it is determined that nothing more can be done, the person's death is managed by professionals. In some communities, there are specialized doctors, hospitals, home care, and hospice dedicated to a person who is dying. Where these exist, the individual can enter the palliative care system designed for an outcome that no longer involves disease-related treatments. Unfortunately, smaller community healthcare systems sometimes don't have these resources. It may take a little effort to seek out what options are available in your area.

I called on nursing homes as a sales representative for four years in the early 1980s. After that I started my own home health medical supply company. That business delivered durable medical equipment and supplies to people's homes. Most of these people were elderly, often with terminal illness. Over the thirty years I worked with all parts of the healthcare system, I never got any indication that death was recognized as anything but a problem to be handed off to the next appropriate professional in the care continuum.

As odd as this may sound, healthcare professionals are not comfortable talking to patients about the prognosis of death. Getting a doctor to talk about the process of dying or even use that term is a conversation you would need to initiate. I recently tried this with my own doctor, and he seemed ill at ease when I said that I didn't want to take a particular drug because I didn't want to chance the side effects. He said he would keep his fingers crossed that I don't die. He seemed perplexed that someone would exchange a better-quality life against the risk of dying.

When we are sick, there is a process filled with specialists, facilities, tests, therapies, and drugs that get placed in our path. When we are identified as dying, this very system that had so many options gets pared down dramatically and becomes more dependent on the person to make decisions about how the process within the system is going to play out. After all, it's called "healthcare". When it becomes death care, options begin to narrow. Some people want to stay in the wellness loop of care and try to be the miracle patient who beats the odds attached to their diagnosis. Others want to enjoy the time they have left, take that last trip, and close out their life on their own terms. These are the two choices available to a person with a terminal diagnosis. Take steps in advance to ensure it's your choice to make.

Thanks to the *Natural Death Act*, which was passed by Congress in 1976, you have more control about how you go out of this world. *Advanced Care Directives* give specific instructions for your family and doctors regarding your personal wishes about end-of-life treatments. If you are going to complete only one of the steps recommended here, I suggest that you download the appropriate forms for an ACD and get the completed documents to your primary care physician, a family member, and whoever will be the executor of your estate such as the designated legal advisor.

MIKE MARABLE

HUNTER'S GOOD DEATH

As I was finishing some updates to send to the publisher of this book, our beloved dog Hunter crossed over to a new adventure. I want to share the experience from my perspective and what transpired two days later when he came to visit me in his spirit form. I wrote this right afterwards, so the memories presented are fresh. It reads the way it unfolded, and I hope it will take you there. His visitation is not surprising. It is a common phenomenon. I anticipated it because Hunter is a skilled traveler himself, as you will discover later in the book.

Sometimes, if you live long enough, you have a few powerful, life-altering experiences. I had one yesterday in assisting Hunter to make his exit out of his old body that no longer was providing him much joy. He let me know in the days before that he was ready. Within the space of my grieving, I can do something for him that is an honor as well as a sacred responsibility.

We spent the days ahead of his planned departure taking in his essence, logging these precious moments in our memories so that we could add them to those gathered over the past sixteen years, all of us grieving in a way that fit our needs. Grief is a way of honoring the loss of the presence of those we love. It can be transforming if allowed to unfold in its full depth, which I have discovered through this experience. Grief for a pet is its own kind of thing and cannot be compared to other types of losses because the relationship is not the same as it is with a friend or family member who have separate lives. A pet's life is dedicated to us, and that bond is forever entangled. There is no right or wrong way to grieve, no timetable. I am immersed in it. It is now one of my teachers.

We made the arrangements that he intuitively told me he wanted and the night before, we invited the other members of his family who had lived in the house at some point and were part of his life. The next morning, we took him to his favorite park, and we sat with him under the tree he had passed a thousand times on walks and playtime there. He took it all in under a perfect blue sky on this sunny fall day.

I arranged for the *Lap of Love* pet hospice to visit us on Saturday, October 21st, 2023. It was scheduled for around 1:00 that afternoon. As per Hunter's wishes, we held his departure ceremony outside in the backyard, one of his favorite places. It is his sacred space; he loves his yard.

He requests a bath in his communication with me, so I carry him outside, and he immediately releases his bowels and bladder. He seems to know what is about to transpire, and he is calm. I filled his pool with water earlier, and it was now perfectly warmed by the sun. I lay him in his pool, and he rests his head against the edge and relaxes into his bath. I gently bathe him and then move him over to the large white cotton quilt laid out next to his pool.

I place him on his left side facing the lemon tree and begin to dry him. Meditation music is playing on my iPhone, and I place a pillow under his head made of folded garments from each of us containing our unique smell. I have his favorite toy brought out, and it is visible to him. The hospice doctor, Analucia, who looks and sounds like an angel as much as any human can, comes and greets him. He looks at her as if he knows her and remains calm. We sit around him and finish drying him with the beach towels he had seen through many baths. The doctor explains what she is doing and what to expect. Hunter remains calm and is taking in the moment. He particularly enjoys this part of bath time, the spa-like pampering he receives.

The doctor gives him a sedative injection which relaxes him even more, and I lie beside him with my head near his. She takes out a white clay mold from her cloth bag and takes an impression of his paw. A symbol of the impression he made on our world. His two moms, Amber and Gayla, gently stroke him, and he locks his eyes on mine. I talk to him softly and gently across the threshold to the next part of his life. Around 1:30, he finishes his beautiful transition, and I am able to be there and gaze directly into his eyes as he does so. It is one of the profound experiences and honors of my life to be able to share in this with him.

Understanding that he is no longer in his body, I look around and begin to talk to him with joy in my voice but tears in my eyes, "You are free, go play".

HOW TO HAVE A GOOD LIFE AFTER YOU'RE DEAD

My back is to the lemon tree, and Gayla excitedly reports a butterfly has arrived and is fluttering around the tree. There are no blossoms; it is not there for the flowers. She tries to get a picture but, before she can, it flies off towards the sky.

We spent the rest of Saturday and Sunday in a bit of a stupor, all of us. One can be as philosophical about losing someone as they like, that is until it happens and much of this goes out the window. I am watching videos on *YouTube* about grief, trying to make sure the feelings I am having are survivable and to see what coping strategies might give some relief from the pain of his loss. The same advice shows up in all of them; let it flow.

That night I slept soundly and don't remember my dreams. Going into the dream world with sadness doesn't help usually and I suspect my unconscious was providing some protection. When I awoke, I didn't feel any better and Gayla took me down to Laguna Beach for breakfast beside the ocean. I ordered a mimosa which usually is a great elixir for any situation. It didn't help. We came home, took naps, watched some football and went to bed early. Intermittently we mentioned Hunter because this is the family space; every inch contains a memory of him.

I fell asleep quickly, got up to drink some water and went back to sleep. Then, the experiences came. Hunter didn't waste any time getting in touch with me. I was willing to dream, and he was waiting for me. I had four successive lucid experiences with him.

Because of my excitement, I had a hard time holding state for very long. It was a fully tactile OBE that started as a dream. I got excited and he was eager to tell me what it was like. Our mutual excitement, while expected, interrupted the encounter as I kept waking up. He looked to be around three or four years old; his coat was fluffy and soft.

My final dream of the morning didn't involve Hunter. I was at an airport and walked through the sliding doors when a man pulled up in a black van next to the entrance. The sliding door on the side was open. It was driven by my friend Jack, who crossed a couple of years ago. His cargo was puppies, maybe twenty of them, all freely climbing around in the van. They looked like Rottweiler puppies, and I greeted them as I walked out. One of them jumped out and I put my face down to his and he took the eyelash of my right eye in his mouth and gently closed his teeth. I awoke from this dream at 7:19, got up to brush my teeth and noticed that a song was playing in my head, "And the dreams I have of dying are the best I ever had".

I remember it's from a *Tears for Fears* song, *Mad World*. I posted in a message to Jack's wife, Michellene. She wrote back to me with this amazing note.

"That is definitely Jack, my hubby; he loved Rotties; he said he would meet up with his two Rottweilers that had also passed". This makes sense now because I didn't know this about Jack, and

HOW TO HAVE A GOOD LIFE AFTER YOU'RE DEAD

Rottweilers are not a breed that I would have chosen for myself. This dream was for both of us it seems. He would know I'd share this with Michellene.

Later that day, Amber told me that she also had an encounter with Hunter in her dream. She said it helped her. As I was waking the next morning and still between worlds, I heard his bark from downstairs. I showered and went down to make coffee. I sensed his presence, and I knew what I needed to do for him, for us. I had a long conversation, directing my gaze towards the spot where I felt him to be in the kitchen. Over the next ten minutes or so I told him of our love and appreciation for all he did for us. He had a unique role in this home. Amber had lost her dad when she was four, and Hunter helped to heal her trauma. He taught me to love, and he comforted Gayla, whose husband had died suddenly many years ago.

Hunter took on a heavy job when he picked this family. I told him it was going to be all right; we would be ok and that he could go. I felt him leave, and I have not felt him or had a dream visit since. This is a painful, but important, ritual. It's important to give them the closure they need, to let them go.

MIKE MARABLE

GET STARTED ON YOUR GOOD DEATH

Most of us want to have the experience of closing our lives out at home in a comfortable setting surrounded by people who care about us. The reality is that the majority of people die in a facility, either a hospital or nursing home. This is a fact, and, like it or not, we may not have that choice if we don't have a plan before the time comes. Our family and friends are not going to prompt us to get our end-of-life plans together, and we shouldn't expect them to. I am doing the prompting for them here, right now. It's time to make peace with inevitability and start making arrangements in the unlikely case that you should drop dead tomorrow or become debilitated by a lingering illness that causes others to intervene and make choices for you.

Because our society finds it difficult to address these matters, we tend to shy away from discussions around death with family members. Part of the process of the good death is letting everyone know what you want. This is not just family but everyone who will be involved in your pre- and post-transition affairs. I have no intention of getting into your personal business here or advising beyond offering some things to consider. For myself, I have created a document that lays everything out in detail. It has all the information that someone might require to assist them in helping close out my life. It's a dynamic document; it must be that way because I change things around frequently, like my account

HOW TO HAVE A GOOD LIFE AFTER YOU'RE DEAD

passwords and PIN numbers, for example. I have included a list of people I want contacted and an email address list. I have simplified my life down to something quite manageable. It takes time, resources, and energy to continuously tend to and maintain all the accumulated stuff over a lifetime. I still have more than I need or use, but it's a work in progress.

My relationships have become leaner, too. I focus on quality over quantity when it comes to where and with whom I spend time.

My partner of nineteen years is my love and companion. I have three good friends who I make sure to talk to or have lunch with every week. I know they will all be there for me when the time comes. I have told them all that I am no tragic figure, and they should celebrate my passing with the same fervor as they would for a friend who won the lottery. They hold what's left of my story. When they leave, any remnants of their version of me will go with them.

My books and writings are scattered around in blogs and are maintained in archives that will be around forever. The internet doesn't purge anything. It won't know I'm not still a potential customer for their advertisers. It's a strange kind of legacy I suppose. *Amazon* will keep on selling my books long after I leave if there is a bank account where the royalties can be deposited. I have left instructions to make sure this continues because I like to think I am leaving some useful information for future generations.

This is a delusion that I allow myself anyway. Used bookstores, *Friends of the Library,* and even yard sales may end up with a copy to sell. I will donate books to libraries, senior centers, and extended care facilities in my area. If someone searches my name by chance in 2100, something will probably come up. I am immortal thanks to technology. The world will never be completely rid of me.

DREAMS AS PRACTICE FOR DYING

If you are wondering what tasks are left for you to complete and wounds left to be healed; you have that information readily available if you want it, through your dreams. In them, you will not only get information about your body and its health but also clues about lingering emotional content that you don't know about. These are the shadows of your unconscious life waiting to be addressed.

You also visit the regions that you will be seeing after you die. Waking, sleeping, dreaming, and dying are not vastly different things.

These are all part of the same gestalt. We tend to think in binary terms about living and dying, yet it is still you having the experience. It comes down to what side of the divide you are having the experience in. When you are asleep and dreaming, part of you separates from your physical body. This second state is the same one you occupy after you die. The only difference is that it no longer has a connection to the body after your heart stops. During sleep, you sometimes travel far into the lands you will occupy after death. You meet your dead relatives or some facsimile of them. You are greeted by well-meaning guides, who give you pointers, and by tricksters who like to have some fun with the naïve dreamers who wander into these places. Mostly, dreamers go to a frequency that is inhabited by other dreamers, so they don't cause problems in other frequencies that are inhabited by those who have taken up residence there after their physical life. These are the consensus realities I write about in a later section. If you learn to become conscious during your dreams, you can gain access to some of these places. You will find there are customs and rules of etiquette that are to be followed.

Dreams make us consciously aware and can help us to unload some of the psychological and emotional baggage accumulated during a lifetime. They are a key ally in our evolution. If you think you have dealt with a situation and yet it keeps presenting itself in waking life, it's not going anywhere. It will likely show up in your dreams. It is your notice, and it offers an opportunity to address it here and now in advance of having to work with it later or prompting another incarnation. These things don't evaporate when we die. If you are reading this book, this may be your notice of it in the waking dream. I am, in a way, your guide during the few hours we are engaged together.

A conscious lifetime, that is, having the knowledge that we are actors in a play, learning about the human experience, is something that can be a gift. Take advantage of it. Deal with your regrets and grievances now, in this reality. Your dreams are telling you about them. Remember this: you are more like who you really are in dreams than the person you pretend to be in polite society. Don't judge yourself for this; work with it. Use this information to better understand yourself. This is what we call "shadow work," bringing the obscured parts of ourselves out into the light of forgiveness and healing.

AFTERWARDS - LIFE STARTS ANEW

The moment after we let out our last breath on this side of the illusory divide, we will immediately enter into the next chapter of an ongoing experience of life.

It may happen suddenly, and you find yourself standing over your physical body wondering what happened. We learn from accounts provided by near-death experiences that this is a common occurrence. If a young person dies in an auto accident, they may find themselves standing outside of their vehicle, thinking they are walking away without a scratch, counting themselves fortunate. They have a body that looks exactly like the one they expect, and the environment is virtually the same one that they move around in every day.

The movie *Ghost* provides a realistic scenario where Patrick Swayze's character in the film is confused about his circumstances after he is murdered in the street. It may dawn on a person that something is amiss when they try to interact with bystanders and get no response. They may hang around the scene and not be fully aware until they realize the driver or passenger in the wrecked car is them. When the ambulance arrives and transports the body to the hospital, they may be inclined to follow it. At some point, however, there is a pull, an uncomfortable sensation that arises the longer one lingers. This is true for anyone in this situation, not just someone who has died unexpectedly. Some try to assert their will and hang around, but it gets increasingly uncomfortable for those who do.

I wish I could tell you exactly what happens for you personally after you die, but I cannot. It is different for everyone. Your experiences will be influenced by many factors. The reality you are going into initially reflects a lifetime of accumulated factors that includes your expectations, hopes, dreams, beliefs, and thought forms that can be both comforting and uncomfortable. It is a mythological land filled with artifacts from your life and culture, along with archetypes from the entirety of the human experience and universal ones that will seem foreign.

In a case where someone went through a prolonged illness, they may have already worked through some of the stages in dreams. A welcoming committee may have assembled and made their presence known in the final days. During the dying process, you may encounter these folks in a vision, or they may appear as real to you as anyone in the physical who might come to visit. As the veil between realities thins with the natural depletion of your life force, you may have experiences that are unexpected for you and those around you. Do not be alarmed if these visitations should occur. Greet your visitors and thank them as you would any human friend. If you are in hospice, your nurses will not be surprised if they see you talking to them. I have discussed this phenomenon with many caregivers over the years, and it is a common occurrence. You might prepare your family that this is a normal phenomenon, so they aren't alarmed or try to get anti-psychotics prescribed. It is all a natural part of the process.

When you figure out you have died, there are initial steps you can take. If there is any question about your situation and you want some verification, try pushing your fingers or fist gently into a wall or the ground. If it goes in, you know you are no longer in Kansas, so to speak. It may be a surprise to you that you don't feel any different or that your surroundings have not changed much. This is because you are used to being a particular person, and that is not going to change abruptly because you died. It would be very disconcerting to suddenly have everything be radically altered from what you are familiar with.

It is common to be greeted upon arrival by family members who went before you and others who are familiar, but you don't quite remember how you know them. You may feel more joy in seeing these people than your relatives. There are reasons for this.

HOW TO HAVE A GOOD LIFE AFTER YOU'RE DEAD

You have been around a lot longer than the short life you just left. You have a lot of catching up to do with old friends you have known over the millennia.

Again, people may think that when they die, the places they go to will be completely foreign lands. More likely, the place you arrive in will have some sense of familiarity for reasons that have been discussed in the dream sections. Remember, you have been through these death experiences many times before. The life you just left was just one of many. You may have a house already designed and built, ready for you to move into, with little memory of being involved in the design. I have been designing mine for years and didn't even know I was doing it until I started waking up there in my bed in dreams. It was happening on another level of my multidimensional awareness. I am not going to get too deeply into this topic in this book. I will leave it for the book coming out next year, delving into the multidimensional, multiplayer aspect of our expanded self.

If by chance you should arrive in a dark place that looks and feels uncomfortable, this is the shadow world that lacks the energy and information to fully constitute itself. It is unlikely, but it happens sometimes when people have not given any thought to what might be awaiting them or don't even believe there is anything after death. If you are in this situation, ask for a light and look around. You will see one; it may be faint and a long way off in the distance, but move towards it. As you get closer ask for assistance, a guide, or a helper. Once you get to the light they will be standing there, if not before. This is true of any situation you might find yourself in; always look for and move towards any light source you see. Light designates a higher frequency or energy. Know this right now, remember it, and don't question what I am about to tell you. Nothing can hurt you. The biggest, baddest, convincing monster can show up (unlikely, but just in case). It absolutely cannot harm you. It is a thought form or a projection of your own fear. You are protected. If you can find love and compassion for anything you see, it is transformed in front of you. Try this in dreams should you remember my words during any encounter you have with these figures. This holds true in the thought responsive worlds of dreams and the realities you encounter after dropping the physical one. If you can learn to become aware that you are dreaming during the dream while you are sleeping, this is a very useful skill to have after you have died. This is called lucid dreaming.

UNDERSTANDING THE LIGHT

If you have a prolonged illness preceding your transition, there is an opportunity to use this time for closing up shop, so to speak. It is our transition preparation time. We are beginning to fade out of this reality stream and have a foot in both worlds. All kinds of dreams will present themselves. Sometimes even scary ones. These should be seen for what they are: the dying of the old self and a clearing out of the remaining baggage. Expect dreams of preparing to move, packing for travel, airplanes, airports, ships, and trains.

People who have near-death experiences get to a particular point in the process where they are greeted by people or by a symbol of their beliefs, such as religious figures. A smaller percentage have a life review. Beyond the life review are some stages that most NDE experiencers don't report. These are reserved for those who are staying. Those of us who have access via out-of-body experiences can be of some assistance here in the plane of reality that you will encounter initially. I call these landing or greeting areas. It has the purpose of helping you understand more about the incarnation you just went through, and to heal and integrate any residual memories and energetic manifestations that you may be holding onto. It is a temporary level. At the appropriate "time," you will know you have to move on to a level that best matches your frequency and the state of your consciousness.

On this side, you are not going to know what that state is, however. It is an accumulation of many lifetimes of learning and evolution. It makes sense that you would believe that your current state of being is an indication, but this is not necessarily so.

You will be presented with options, at some point, following the life review. You may think you know how you would choose; the reality is that you can't know because you will have a different perspective than you now have. Guidance will be provided, but your free will is never interfered with. It will be your decision. As you choose, you will see varying degrees of intensity in the light portals. Some may appear to be too bright, too intense; you will know intuitively which one is right for you and your stage of evolution. It will feel comforting and accepting. Your energy will match this light, and you will step into it to begin participating in your choices. I cannot tell you what is beyond this because we who travel remain on this side of that light. There is nothing to be afraid of. There is no judgment, only love and acceptance, no matter who you are or what you did in this lifetime. You were like an actor in a movie, and you played some parts; that's all it was.

KEEPING AN OPEN CURIOUS MIND AFTER DEATH

I think about all the NDE research that is available now; it provides opportunities to absorb information about what happens after we die that our ancestors could never have dreamed of. The opportunity to openly discuss and consider that consciousness continues to learn and evolve independent of the physical body and brain is important information for society to have. At the very least, it gets people to question their assumptions and cultural biases. Looking more deeply into any subject helps us gain knowledge and perspective. As the number of experiences grows, it gets much harder to deny the reality of these events.

HOW TO HAVE A GOOD LIFE AFTER YOU'RE DEAD

This preponderance of anecdotal evidence tells us that an afterlife exists. We can compare it in some ways to the UAP phenomenon, where governments around the world have been forced to acknowledge UAP existence after years of denial. Any science that completely dismisses the non-locality of consciousness is standing on a progressively flimsy platform where this kind of denial begins to look anti-scientific.

Because these experiences are subjective, our biases don't disappear after we die. Our strong beliefs that penetrate our identity will often accompany us.

It makes sense if you think about it. We hold onto the personalities from the life we just lived for a while. For example, let's take accounts from near-death experiences where some people report encounters with religious figures and others don't. This is an indicator of subjective content and expectations inserting themselves into the interpretations of the people who experience these things. If we see a being or encounter a thought form that resembles our expectations, be it heaven, angels, Jesus, Mohammad, or even God, we can assign it a meaning that fits our belief model. Studies around the world have identified how societal/cultural influences impact these experiences. This is built into the process, and for very practical reasons it seems. It could be disconcerting to be faced with the starkness of a very different reality than expected following our physical death. There is no harm in these illusions. They can be sorted out later if the person is interested in doing so. There is never any push to change a person's mind about their personal interpretations.

Many of us with an interest to do so travel via the OBE state into some of the regions people occupy after physical death. Just as Swedenborg noticed, we find that people who have things in common often share a particular community. For example, religious ideologies have their own "zones." These areas can be quite limited, with some resembling giant movie sets about the size of a large theme park. It appears that there are as many of these consensus realities as there are strongly held beliefs and lifestyle preferences. Many of the inhabitants eventually figure out that this isn't optimal, or they may get bored and move on from these regions. Those who are happy in their situation are given the opportunity to reincarnate from these areas if they like. They often go back into a life where these beliefs systems are perpetuated within families and circumstances with which they are familiar. This can make for a slower evolutionary journey.

I write this not to challenge anyone's belief system or to push a particular theory about an afterlife. I don't have a dog in the fight or feel any urge to try to change people's minds. This information is just what I and others have noticed when we visit these places and ask questions. I continue to try to question the world around me, and I challenge any cultural conditioning, ideologies, and beliefs that I have integrated into my personal identity. There is way more going on than any institution,

HOW TO HAVE A GOOD LIFE AFTER YOU'RE DEAD

philosophy, science, or religion has scratched the surface on, much less figured out. If you read any book by travelers like me, including this one, that tries to tell you exactly how it all works, remember that these experiences are heavily influenced by both conscious and unconscious conditioning. We who do this must be careful not to buy into our experiences without questioning them.

I think the most important takeaway from this is that we be aware that our consciousness does indeed survive physical death. Maintain your curiosity and openness to all possibilities, both on this side and after you cross over. Don't reflexively buy into any illusion that may be projected in front of you as it may be from your own mind or is just there waiting for your belief vibration, whether it be an angel or a monster.

With this mindset, you can maintain the freedom to explore all the potential that is offered in your post-human experience. Keep asking questions. Call for guides and find the optimal set of circumstances available to you, given your level of consciousness. Stay curious.

MIKE MARABLE

I See Dead People (and try to lend them a helping hand)

When I first started moving around outside of my physical body and traveling, I would venture outside in the dark of the night. As I walked around on what seemed to be a version of the street in front of my house, I saw people walking around. Some appeared to be in a stupor or trance like state. Others looked like they were engaged in socializing like you might expect to see at a block party. On occasion, one would come up to me and ask a question, such as, had I seen a particular person they were looking for or how to get home.

I figured out early on that some of these are dead folks who hadn't moved on past the lower level closest to the earth frequency. Others are still living and out doing what they normally do while their body is home sleeping and dreaming. This was the beginning of my trying to help these earthbound people get on with their transition and move to a place where they might find their way to get on track to complete their afterlife journey. I had no experience or qualifications in this area, but intuitively surmised that I needed to somehow get them to a higher frequency, closer to the light.

I did this for a couple of years, sort of flying by the seat of my pants and testing what methods worked better than others. I would get frustrated sometimes because there were so many, and I couldn't get to all of them. One time, I rounded up a group of them and got them to run up a hill towards a group of lights in the sky and watched them one by one get airborne and shoot up in the air as if pulled up by an invisible bungee cord. Little blips of incandescence would flash in the dark sky as they disappeared into the lights. One woman ran by me, turned back to thank me, and then flew off like the others.

Over time, they would come to me in the house. I sometimes wondered if I was part of some sort of afterlife referral program. In the early 1990s, I attended two programs at *The Monroe Institute* (TMI). It was during one of these weeks that I came to understand and verify that in fact, these were people who had not moved on. There were people associated with TMI who had been assisting these folks for many years.

An educational program had been personally created by Robert Monroe with the express purpose of training people like me who had the ability to reach them in the OBE state. The *Lifeline* program, as it was aptly named, had established defined protocols and a best practices approach that would better ensure success with more consistent outcomes for getting people into better circumstances that might allow a completed transition. My class contained people from all walks of life; some were healthcare professionals and hospice nurses.

I was surprised as I sat in the first gathering to see Elisabeth Kubler Ross, MD, the renowned doctor on the topic of death and dying. It would be like showing up for music class and finding out Paul McCartney was one of your classmates.

We learned from the instructors some of the reasons that people stick around the earth level after they die. Through their experiences in doing this work, in what they referred to as "retrievals," they had enough conversations with earthbound people to better understand what happens. They helped us come up with our own interview questions. Their findings revealed that most of these earthbound individuals either didn't know or had forgotten that they had died. Some were afraid to leave because they were worried that they might face judgment for the things they had done in the life just led. There were also incidents of unfinished affairs and concerns about the loved ones they didn't want to leave behind. The interviewers also discovered something surprising: earth life can be addictive. It turns out that just because someone dies doesn't mean the cravings naturally go away. Cigarettes, alcohol, sex, and other drugs can maintain their hold on someone even after their physical body is no longer present.

HOW TO HAVE A GOOD LIFE AFTER YOU'RE DEAD

Because of the proximity to the earth vibration, a person can hang around living people with a similar addiction and get some of the residual effects.

The impact of this parasitic relationship can be detrimental to both parties, affecting the health and wellbeing of the living person and preventing the person who died from moving on.

I left that class relieved to learn that there was an actual need for my unusual skills within this very specialized kind of work. I felt more competent and relaxed with the notion that I could do this work without screwing it up and doing more harm than good. Another feeling arrived that I didn't expect, and that was gratitude. I was honored to be trusted to do this work.

One of the most important things I have learned that makes for a successful retrieval (also called a "rescue") is how to work with guides, also known as helpers. There are unlimited helpers on the other side whose job in that realm is to assist people to get to where they are supposed to be following physical death. With their assistance, I find I can deliver a person to a frequency level where the guide can make them feel more comfortable with the idea of moving on. The guides' methods are both brilliant and comical.

You may have the question in mind as to why the guides seek human involvement in these rescue operations. As it was explained to me, we who are still having the Earth life can be "seen" in the lower frequencies because we are from a denser frequency than they are. At these levels, guides are harder to see for the person who has died, just as we can't normally see ghosts or our own helpers. Another reason is that we are more relatable to the person who has died. They just came from the earth frequency; we give off a certain signature energy that feels familiar.

The guides have alluded to why I have this assignment, and they have complimented me on occasion for having the right temperament for this work. Because I seem to have an intuitive understanding of what to do, I get the feeling that this was one of my missions when coming into this life. Of course, I proceed in a caring way; and yet I don't get emotionally engaged because it is difficult to stay in the necessary state in the presence of intense emotion. I tend to take the attitude of what an emergency medical technician (EMT) or emergency room doctor might have. I must stay focused on the task, get the job done, and then move on. Another essential skill necessary to carry this out is to be able to hold state in an OBE long enough to finish the retrieval. I rarely lose someone mid retrieval and, when it does happen, it is upsetting. I feel as if I let them down. I always go looking for them and fortunately usually find them. If I can stay focused and have reserve energy, I will hang around and see if I can learn something from the guides.

Over the years, I have learned that there is a long history of this service—that escorting those who left this earth to safely reach the other side of the river is a sacred practice going back

HOW TO HAVE A GOOD LIFE AFTER YOU'RE DEAD

thousands of years. Oral histories speak of indigenous cultures and their Shamans who travel with the departed to help ensure their safe arrival into the afterlife. There were also the psychopomps in Ancient Greek society, and today we have soul midwives, *Death Doulas* and *Death Walkers*. These traditions continue to be maintained in our modern society. There is also a growing number of organizations supporting a more conscious death process, understanding that the nature of life and death is not separate but part of the whole. This is something that we all are working towards understanding in our own way. It is the primary theme running throughout this book.

MIKE MARABLE

Retrievals And Other Experiences

MY FATHER'S TRIP TO THE LIGHT

In western cultures, there is a reticence about death and the dying process. This is particularly true here in the United States, where people "battle" terminal illness as if it was a war to win or lose. We may hear that someone lost a battle with a disease like cancer. I don't think that kind of language is particularly helpful. Cancer is the number one cause of death in America. Human bodies produce thousands of cancer cells daily, and the immune system addresses most of them, but as we get older, our immune systems are not as efficient. We all have cancer cells; it is a natural phenomenon. Toxins in the environment, stressors and other exacerbating agents can impact our vulnerability, but these are often unavoidable in modern society.

My dad died of pancreatic cancer in 2013. He and I had discussed his transition as his time was winding down. The last time I saw him, I told him that I would see him again--that he couldn't go somewhere that I couldn't find him.

He said confidently, with a smile, "Well, I certainly hope so!". I didn't know if he meant that he thought he would still be around in this life to see me or understood my reference that I would find him on the other side. I never abandoned some optimism that he might make it. Miracles do happen, though not that often, with this kind of cancer.

Over the years, I shared with him my out-of-body adventures. He always listened patiently and didn't ask too many questions. I always wondered what he really thought about my stories. One night at dinner with some of his friends, out of nowhere, he said rather proudly, "Mike has out-of-body experiences." I was taken aback by his announcement. The person sitting next me during dinner later asked me about them. Let's face it, it's an odd thing to talk about at a dinner party. I have never discussed it with any other medical professionals except my dad's hospice nurse during his final days. I wanted her to understand that I had talked to him about things like this. I was also feeling her out to see what her openness might be around this topic.

Hospice personnel are exposed to all kinds of things that could be interpreted as supernatural phenomena. His nurse was not only receptive, but she also wanted to know more. I have stayed in contact with her since his passing. As he reached the end, he slept most of the time, and his doctor regularly increased his pain medication.

I last saw my father in person during Thanksgiving week in 2013. I live in California, and he is in Virginia. Two nights before Thanksgiving Day, he was able to summon the energy to go to dinner with me at his favorite restaurant. The next night, we were in the emergency room. He spent that night in the hospital, and I picked him up. He was in good spirits, so we went to a friend's home for an afternoon Thanksgiving dinner. He fell asleep on the couch, sitting up; this was expected. People who are getting ready to leave sleep a lot. I was told they are getting acclimated to their new environment. Not unlike how babies sleep a lot, they have a foot in both worlds after they arrive here. It seems that is true for people getting ready to go out.

My dad and stepmother Trudy celebrated their 50th wedding anniversary on December 21st. The assisted living center where they lived had arranged a room for them to have a private dinner. He had been moved to the healthcare section of the facility by now, and they brought him down for this very special occasion. They adored each other more than I have ever witnessed two people in love.

On December 26th, 2013, Waverly Hobson Marable Jr. began his journey on the other side of the veil.

His memorial service was to be on that following Thursday, and I immediately got on a plane to make my way back to Virginia. I stayed with a family friend at their home the night before his Celebration of Life service. Dad and Trudy had planned out every specific detail for each of their respective services years in advance. The facility, speakers, music, and reception were all ready to go

HOW TO HAVE A GOOD LIFE AFTER YOU'RE DEAD

right down to the selected plates and napkins. This is not an exaggeration; it is how they lived their lives, and little was left to chance. People who lived through the depression era know what it feels like to be caught off guard by circumstances.

I awoke the morning of the service early; it wasn't light out yet. Knowing it was going to be a long demanding day on my energy, I went back to sleep. Almost immediately, I was consciously aware of being in a totally dark space illuminated only by the ambient light of a man standing with a red blanket-like covering from his shoulders down to his calves. He was naked and was pulling it around him as if trying to stay warm. He was young, maybe late twenties.

He had curly dark hair, the style Tony Curtis wore in the 1940s. As I got closer, I recognized who it was from pictures I had seen of my father when he was holding me as a baby. It was my father. Realizing I needed to work quickly before I lost my control over this OBE state (emotions can cause someone to "blink out" and wake up), I instinctively knew what to do. He was in a dream-like stupor, so I made eye contact with him and said, "Dad, wake up". He looked at me, and a slight sense of recognition registered on his face as if to say, "What's going on?". I said, "Dad, it's Mike; I need you to listen to me, ok?". He then looked down, getting his bearings and said, "It's so cold". The thought came to me that maybe he hadn't been cremated yet. A light came from behind me over my right shoulder and illuminated his face. He was becoming lucid to his situation. With this, I lifted him up in my arms and hoisted him up in the air. He began to float up into the darkness. The only light in this space was the ambient light being given off by the two of us. He rose higher to what looked like fifty feet above me. He then took off like a rocket to an altitude where clouds might be in an earthly sky. A round opening in the darkness appeared with the colors of the rainbow. I watched him fly through it. The whole event, from when I discovered him in this dark space to his exiting through this opening, seemed like two minutes. I knew I had to move fast to get it done and keep my emotions under control. It felt like an emergency where one just reacts and somehow does the right things.

I have been to see him on multiple occasions since, and he comes into my dreams, which almost always triggers my lucidity. We have short but meaningful conversations. Not as father and son so much as peers who shared a life together. I later attended his second death ceremony and these visitations stopped.

TRAVELS TO THE OTHER SIDE

I tend to look at OBEs and lucid dreams in the same category of non-local events. I am not sure, but I suspect that most of my lucid dreams originate as an out-of-body experience. I had an OBE last night in which I helped two women transition. They were related, a mother and daughter.

HOW TO HAVE A GOOD LIFE AFTER YOU'RE DEAD

Hospice workers work on one side, and those of us who can help on the other side. I wish people were better prepared for what happens when their heart stops beating and they stop breathing-- what we call physical death. They are immediately awake in the next moment in an unfamiliar territory; some have no idea what happened. Pre-death dreams, whether remembered or not, help in preparing someone for this. They are often receiving helpful information from those they trust. Experiencing the presence or dreams of loved ones prior to transitioning is common. Ask any hospice nurse. If patients are heavily medicated for pain with morphine-derived drugs, it can interfere with the natural transition process. They won't dream properly.

In some cases, I can get them close enough vibrationally that I can watch them from a distance go through the opening of the portal. What an honor that is! There is an opening, a blip of light, and then it closes back up. It's pretty much always the same. One time, I helped a group of people, and they all went through in succession. When they saw the light, they ran up a hill towards it. It's always dark in these situations, and I look for a light that I can take them to. I also try to take them upward to be able to see it. I conclude this to metaphorically mean I take them up to a place where the vibrations are higher. I could hear some of them say, "there it is," as they took off in flight and would disappear in blips of light as they went through the portal. One elderly woman with white hair passed me but turned around to thank me before she became airborne. That was one of the more memorable ones. Some don't want to go.

Most of the time, I get them to what I call a "way station." these are higher vibrational locations that may appear to the person as familiar so that it is of some comfort to them. They all look different, but even though we are in this dark space, there will be an amber-hued oasis in the dark. Sometimes they meet people they know or recognize and then go off with them. I sometimes hang around and chat with the guides there. This scene was set up as a garage where you work on cars, complete with cars with the hoods up. I recognized one of the guides I had seen at other locations. We shook hands, and he acknowledged that we had met many times.

What made this experience a little different was that in the transport of the mother, I slipped back to awareness in my bed. I knew, having done this so many times, that I could immediately get back out, so as I went out of the window to try to find the mother, the daughter was there too. I took her to a way station that looked like a garage and handed her over. I then went to find the mother.

I saw her floating in the inky blackness, so I navigated her back to the garage. The mother and daughter greeted each other. Having a little fun with them, I told them this was heaven. They looked surprised. I said yes because they were naughty and didn't move on as they should have, this was their heaven. I told them they shouldn't hang around the living, taking their energy. I sensed they knew exactly what they had done, so I asked the daughter, "What did you learn about me?". She said she knew I was a writer.

There are some differences between this kind of experience and a lucid dream or regular OBE. First, in the OBE, it is usually dark with an amber-like light that might be around a person or a location. Outside of that space, it is inky darkness. Although I start off taking them from a location at night that is dark, it may be lit by moonlight. When I get them to a way station, it is in this inky dark space.

Another difference is the presence of beings I meet in OBEs, whom I call guides. They, like me, are volunteers, there to help the people. Unlike dream characters, they have complete conversations with me and are doing a job. They are polite but often matter of fact about the task. I always try to better understand their work. As in this case, sometimes there is one I have met before. Who knows, he may be my guide, not theirs.

RETRIEVAL OF JASON N.

When doing a retrieval, the ones that get to me the most are the kids.

I read about a suicide yesterday. A Facebook friend whom I don't know personally wrote that her son had killed himself that day. Realizing that timing is of the essence in these cases, I made the decision to see if I could find him. I had his name, and she posted pictures of him. He appeared to be in his mid-20s.

When I want to increase my chances of having an OBE, there is a flower extract supplement that I take that does it for me. It helps keep the waking mind lucid and online especially during long and stable experiences. This is essential for retrievals. I can't take the chance of blinking out at a critical moment. In this friend's case, I stayed the course for the retrieval and remained in a stable state for hours.

As I initially roll out, I hear a child say, "Mom!". I don't know what to think about this at the time, but I soon find out. I get out into my room, and I feel someone grab me. It's dark, but I can make out the features. It's a small boy, maybe four or five years old. I ask him his name, and he says, "Jason." I have only helped children a dozen or so times in my 34 years of doing this. I move quickly to get him somewhere that I can find a helper guide to take him. I go downstairs and out the front door. I call out for someone to assist, but nothing happens. I figure I am in a dense environment and maybe am in a low frequency myself. If the guides are there, I can't see them.

I get airborne with him, trying to find a location that has some light. The presence of light indicates a frequency change. I stop at a place and sit him down on a sofa, and we start talking. I ask him where he lived and his last name. Both are answered quickly and clearly. I ask if he knew how he died, and he explains that he was doing something he wasn't supposed to, and something fell on him.

I see the story of what happened to him in my mind. When I come back from this mental side trip, he is gone. There is a tall, skinny man with long blond hair there, and I ask where Jason is. He says, "Oh, he's probably around here somewhere, running around. I wouldn't worry." I intuitively don't trust him and go looking for Jason in this house. The man and a couple of other characters start trying to block me and come towards me in a menacing way. I go around them and find him. As I am looking for him, I see various boys, mostly pre-teen-aged kids, milling aimlessly around. It dawns on me what these dark characters are. They collect young boys. Yes, folks, there are predators in the lower astral. Death does not change some people. Addictions and bad impulses can remain, and there are places where these people reside. I am thinking that I may be stopped in a lower astral realm while trying to get my bearings.

My delay in getting him to safety could have been disastrous. I pick him up, fly out a window, and set my intention. I get to a much better-lit place, and I know I can get a helper here. I ask for assistance, and immediately see a kindly-looking woman coming through a door. I take him over to her, and she takes him into the kitchen. He then runs to someone and calls out, "Nanna!" It may be his grandmother or a representation of her. I am soon joined by others who know him. One seems to be his mother. It could be she is in a dream and is trying to visit him. I can only assume that this is the case, however. She doesn't seem lucid to the circumstances, and having her son still alive is not a surprise to her. I take this to mean she is visiting us in a non-lucid dream. I look her squarely in the eyes and tell her that she will remember all of this in the morning. Jason's Nanna takes him over to the astral refrigerator in the kitchen, and he sees something he wants. It turns out to be pumpkin bars—like pumpkin pie but in square bars.

We all sit down and talk while we eat the bars. They taste exactly like pumpkin pie. I am thinking this is a representation of his kitchen at home, and these bars are something he likes. I can't help myself from bringing up how interesting it is that all of us are here in an astral reality eating a delicious desert. I stop to listen to their conversations with each other. I am the only one there who doesn't know any of the others. It has the feeling of a party or reunion around the table. I tell them I must get going. One of them thanks me and mentions what a valuable skill this is that I have. I tell her that it is a great honor to help Jason. I then immediately wake up in my bed.

IMPRESSIONS: I need to find a better way to ensure that I get someone's assistance promptly. I was at a very dense level close to the earth and had trouble getting the frequency high enough to be able to see the helper. This could have gone south for me and for Jason. OK is not good enough.

I understand that it can be disconcerting to think that children can also be in these situations. I was surprised of this as a possibility when I first encountered a child. I also understand that parents who read this account may dismiss it and I think this is a perfectly reasonable response. I will add that I do not see children very often in these regions. It is rare, but it does happen. Children are curious and are predisposed to look for help. This would greatly assist them to be able to exit these regions. They also don't have the psychological baggage and belief systems that adults may carry. After all, no one is truly stuck in these frequencies. Most people figure it out eventually and leave. Children have a high frequency level and would not normally inhabit these areas to begin with. There are helpers everywhere and this is particularly true for children I suspect.

MIKE MARABLE

DEAD FOLKS TELL ME WHY THEY STAY

Way back, when I first started to get out of my body, I would run into dead people. Being a helpful person by nature, I would try to see if they needed any assistance. Back then, I didn't know much about the different vibratory levels and why some people don't move on. Later, I attended the Lifelines Program at The Monroe Institute and became more familiar with these concepts. (Robert Monroe was alive then, and Elizabeth Kubler Ross was in my class there in Faber, Virginia). So, for 30 years or so, I have been escorting people to a place where a guide can help them get to the light, or whatever it is they do. I just get them that far. I have learned that at certain frequency levels, we who are still alive can have an advantage in getting a dead person's attention because we are dense enough that they can see us. Guides are less likely to be seen because they vibrate at a higher frequency. We can't see "ghosts" for this reason. In our physical form, we are locked into this frequency within our natural state of consciousness.

This year, I sort of took a break from my retrieval psychopomp work. I took the mirror out of my room, which I think had something to do with many of my encounters. I hadn't had one in about 8 months. The other night, I saw Bruce Moen's book on this subject in my book stack and pulled it out. Bruce is the only person I know of who wrote about his retrieval experiences. Like me, he attended the Lifelines Program. I re-read a chapter or two.

HOW TO HAVE A GOOD LIFE AFTER YOU'RE DEAD

(I learned that he had transitioned by the time I originally bought the book). This got my subconscious thinking about retrievals and last night I got out. I found myself outside in the dark with only the ambient light of the night sky to guide me. I saw some people. I asked them if they were dead, and they said yes. I tend to be direct in my questions because I don't know how much time I have in this state. If they know they are dead, I handle it differently because they can be a more difficult case. It often means they have chosen to stick around.

A woman broke off from the group. She seemed kind of interested in me, and I told her what I do. She was reluctant to believe me and asked if I had any "credentials." I politely said, "Come with me," and she let me take her hand. I called out to the darkness, "I'd like a guide to help with this one." Nothing happened so I tried again. On the third occasion, I saw a transparent form take shape and then become completely visible. I suspect that my intention had raised my frequency up enough that I could see the guide, who was in the form of a woman. She then quickly changed her appearance, and the woman I retrieved seemed to recognize her. The two went off together. I have seen this before, where the guide makes themself more familiar to the person. This happens sometimes as well when people are greeted in their NDEs. Grandma may not actually be Grandma; rather, it's a representation of her that contains aspects of the personality. I have no way of knowing how this is achieved.

I figured my work was done and walked back to where I had originally met the woman. This is where I encountered a group of men sitting on long benches that made a kind of semi-circle. The ambient light of their life force lit the area enough so I could see them quite clearly.

I was in a very stable OBE, and I stopped to address them as a group. They all acknowledged that, yes, they were aware they had died. I looked around and clearly saw each face. They were in a variety of states of disheveled appearances and clothes. Some looked sick, and one didn't have a head but was talking in a very animated fashion. After all, it's all telepathic communication, so I guess one doesn't need a head. Another man stuck a syringe in his neck and then seemed to spit in his shirt pocket. Not quite as strange as the cast of the movie *Beetlejuice*, but as close as I want to see. I asked them why they stay here. I got a variety of very cogent answers, rationalizations that their lives in this state weren't bad. They seemed to enjoy each other's company.

One guy with long hair and a mustache appeared like he was from the 1970s and was holding a beer glass that was half full. He said that he wanted to be able to drink beer and "chase quality poon." I asked if he had gotten any "poon" lately. He laughed and said no, he hadn't.

I then blinked out of this and woke up in my bed. I lay there running back through the events to make sure I remembered them and what had just happened. My feeling in talking to them was that this was the life they knew.

In life, some people don't care about having a different experience either. There are those who have no interest in traveling to another country, attending a play, or going to a high-end hotel or restaurant. They like their life just the way it is. I wonder if this is what happens when a person with this mindset dies? I remember reading an article once about how many homeless people are very satisfied by not reentering into society. We seem to think life is best conducted through a career, home ownership and a nice car. There are others, maybe like these guys, who don't care about another kind of existence. They like the life they are leading just fine.

MIKE MARABLE

GROUP MOVE TO A HIGHER FREQUENCY

I had this experience last week, and it is still one I am thinking about. After a series of OBEs, I had a false awakening and was trying to get out of my room to another locale. I have been recovering from a virus, and, while my OBE activity hasn't been impacted, I have had a more difficult time getting out of the local and lower settings. In this case, it resulted in an extraordinary experience. Though short, it remains most memorable.

I find myself in what looks like a homeless encampment. It is light but under a gray sky, so it is not really in the very lowest, darker astral regions, but it is not pleasant. The people look disheveled, and their living conditions are squalid. I encounter a group of men and women and ask if they would like to go somewhere better. They talk among themselves and agree that yes, they would. I have no idea how I know to do this; it just comes to me, and I ask them to gather around me in a group hug. I instruct them to love each other, even if there are members of the group they don't like. I then ask them to send love to each other, and I would do the same. It seemed as if twenty or more join the group hug, and then everything goes dark. Almost immediately, all of us are now standing in beautiful fields and green grass plains near a lake surrounded by mountains. It reminds me of the fields where Julie Andrews danced and sang in the movie *The Sound of Music*. Much to my amazement, all the people's appearances had dramatically changed. They now look as if they had just visited a spa and hired a stylist. I remembered, upon waking, that Jurgen Ziewe discussed in his books how people become more attractive and youthful in the higher frequency regions.

I think being surprised in these experiences is important feedback and is a form of validation. In this one, almost everything was unexpected. I didn't plan on doing the group hug. I have never considered it or had done one previously. I have never visited a place resembling the original setting or where we ended up. I just sort of got the idea and went with it.

RETRIEVAL OF DEB C – A CASE VERIFIED

I roll out and find a woman in my bedroom standing in the dark. I suspect she followed me back from an earlier OBE. I take her downstairs out the front door into the dark night. I see her face. She is around 5'4". She appears to be in a dream-like state, and, as we walk, she is coming out of her stupor. I ask her some questions. Her name is Deb. She has lived in various places, the last being New Jersey. I ask for her last name, but it has multiple syllables. I now can't remember it, but it starts with a "C". When I ask for her address, she gives me her email address. Such are the times we live in. I explain what is happening and that if for some reason I lose her or disappear, she is to look for a light and someone will help her. I then ask for a light and a guide to assist Deb.

We turn the corner on the street, and almost immediately we arrive at a makeshift way station with what looks like portable industrial lighting set up on what you might find on a movie set. There is a card-like table about twenty feet long, and people are sitting down assisting other arrivals. It's dark all around us, but this area is lit brightly. I get the attention of one of them who seems to be in charge, and I tell her that I need some help for Deb. She tells me in a formal tone that I need to wait. They do seem to have their hands full.

I turn to Deb to ask her when her death happened. One of the guides looks at me and says, "This morning." I ask Deb what happened. She tells me that she was painting, and a fire started. As she is telling me this, she transforms into a woman who looks to be in her 50s or 60s. Her face is charred on the left side as if it is blackened by the smoke. She seems a little embarrassed by the incident. I think to myself that this must have been awful for her, but she seems to take it in stride.

I get her to sit down and ask her if she is religious. She says no, and so I tell her that no matter what she may have heard, there is no judgement here. The only judgement we might experience is that we impose on ourselves. I explain that she can let those feelings go as they are not necessary here. I feel myself starting to fade and tell her I must go. She says that it's ok.

I fully wake up in my bed and think about writing this event down. It is about 5 AM. I have it committed firmly to memory, so I decide to go back to sleep. After some restful sleep, I find myself in the place they took Deb. They have her doing something. I then see others that I recognize. These people also conduct retrievals. I know them, and I even remember a couple of their names. I am so happy to see them all there together.

This has never happened before, that I remember. We all sit down together at a square table that looks like something one might find in a kitchen. We all are laughing and happy to reunite. I recognize a woman and two of the guys as guides who have previously come to help with some of my retrievals. It has a bit of a dinner party atmosphere. I express how good it is to find people "like me", meaning others that do this work.

I tell them that I feel stable and can stay awhile, and one of them asks me if I would like to be "bi-lingual". I don't know exactly what they mean but say that I am game. We get up and go to another table where there is something I am supposed to ingest. I assume this is going to help me with whatever this bi-lingual thing is. I don't ask a lot of questions about it because I don't want to fade out before I receive the benefit of whatever gift it is they are offering to me when I return to my body. It doesn't taste very good. I ask if I must eat the whole thing, which is a gooey slab about the size of a slice of cheesecake. They are amused that I just dived in. I tell them I am the adventurous kind, and they laughed at my response.

It is time for me to go. I walk back and say goodbye to the guides and to the woman, who, I sense arranged this for us. I thank and hug her. She says something along the lines that some of these people would be moving on, so this will be the last time. I understand her meaning and say yes, we will move on soon. I meant some of them would be graduating either from the human, reincarnating, etc. She smiles and doesn't say anything. I say, "I understand you can't talk about that." I immediately wake up around 7:15 AM and write down this amazing experience that I will cherish forever.

NOTES: This was a fascinating experience, and it got more interesting because I looked Deb up. I had the approximate date, where she had lived and a sense of her last name. It was recent, and I thought that the details of it being a fire might give me what I needed to track her down. I felt that I was successful in finding her so then went to her *Facebook* page, which was still active, to see if I could get any more details. I learned that she was the mother of three daughters. I asked my partner if maybe I should contact them. She didn't think this was a good idea, and I agreed. The important thing is that she is safe.

DOGS IN THE AFTERLIFE

My boy Hunter turned sixteen this September. I get asked if dogs have an afterlife. I don't know if all do, obviously, but I see

HOW TO HAVE A GOOD LIFE AFTER YOU'RE DEAD

enough dogs in my travels that I know some do. I have read NDE accounts where people have met with their own pets, and I have watched an NDE *YouTube* video where pets were reported as having been seen over there.

In my experiences with Hunter, he does have a second-state appearance, what some call an astral body. I have mentioned in my writings that when we had his bed in our bedroom, before we moved it downstairs due to his age, he would greet me with his astral body when I got out. I would sometimes take him with me. He got proficient enough at it that he learned to follow me on his own when I went out the window in the bedroom.

Last week, I got out and went downstairs, and his astral doggie-self greeted me. I was surprised to learn that he had a cat, of all things, sitting on his bed. As far as I know, he has never seen a cat. Somehow, he had made friends with an astral cat. Some cats grow up with dogs, so it could be that this one was out traveling and followed Hunter back.

It is my understanding that some pets can reincarnate if they want to. They, like us, have more awareness of circumstances in that state and can make choices. I asked the question that I have always wondered, "Can pets reincarnate into a human life?" It was explained that some do, and that they will pick situations and families where they can learn the ways of being human and have more responsibilities to help them prepare. The circumstances are arranged for an appropriate setting for this to occur. I don't know if this is the case for Hunter specifically, but his intelligence and the awareness level he exhibited, along with his keen observance of us, suggests that he may be planning to give a human lifetime a try. In any case, I feel comfortable that he will have an afterlife, as he has some advance knowledge of the areas one goes to.

ADDENDUM: There are pet hospice organizations that will help the family and the pet. There are vets who do the euthanasia in the home setting. Please, to all reading this, don't drop a pet off or have them die alone. You can talk to your pet about what is going to happen. They understand way more than you think they do. You can ask your guides to greet them. Our pets are very special companions whom we love and who love us unconditionally. The Lap of Love pet hospice program has participating veterinarians across the country.

HOW TO HAVE A GOOD LIFE AFTER YOU'RE DEAD

A PARK WITH CHILDREN AND DOGS

I roll out and raise my frequency. I find myself in a park area with children, dogs, and care givers. I am lucid and in what appears to be a special consensus reality stream. I love dogs, and I begin interacting with some. They are very playful and affectionate. I start walking around the park, and a young girl, maybe six years old, joins me and walks with me. I am surprised as she takes my hand. I have nothing against children, but given the choice, I prefer the company of the dogs better. I didn't decide to have children during my current earth visit and haven't regretted it, but I like this little girl. Later, as I leave, I kneel to say goodbye, and she starts talking to me about how her father is gone and that she wants to find him. I tell her that I hope she finds him. She seems determined.

I then find myself in a take-out kind of restaurant; there are seats at a long counter like you see in diners. I see there is a woman and a young girl, about eight years old is my guess. She has strawberry blonde hair in a pixie cut and she is sitting a couple of stools down from me. She is chatting up the person behind the counter and is very funny. I listen to her for a couple of minutes and say to her, "You must be the world's shortest stand-up comedian...you are hilarious!"

She looks over at me, checks me out up and down and says, "And you're old!" I laugh, and then we get along great, talking and laughing for what seems like twenty minutes. The person with her had moved to a table and has now come back to get her. We had bonded in the time we spent together, and I tell her it's likely we won't see each other again. She agrees and gives me a kiss on the cheek. I will always remember that little girl whom I met from who knows where and her amazing sense of humor and intelligence.

WOMAN WHO WAS MURDERED

Last night was a wild night. I conducted a retrieval of a woman who was murdered, and I met her assailant. It then started off a series of dreams and lucid dreams on the topic of murder itself.

I wake up at 1:35 and look at the clock. It's a full moon. I don't know if that makes any difference regarding altered states, but it is always my expectation that it will, so possibly it is self-fulfilling. Either way, it works.

I fall back to sleep quickly, and, within what seems like minutes, I wake up in my subtle body and sense that I can roll out. As I try to get out, I feel some hands around me. They are holding on tightly. I have some difficulty getting them off. It is a woman in her late twenties with long dark hair. (Age doesn't reveal anything as they all look about this age.) I can see her face in the ambient light of our bedroom. I take her out of the bedroom window and we land outside the house. I ask her how she found me, and she says she followed me back from a store she saw me in. This conversation moves us to a different location where there is some light. I ask her if she knows that she had died, and she says yes. I then ask how, and she says that she was murdered.

This is only the third murder case I have dealt with that I am aware of. Sometimes the people don't remember how they died or don't want to reveal it. I ask her to tell me about it and the next thing I know, we are in the room. There is another person with us, a male. I understand intuitively that it is her assailant. I have no idea if I am in the room with his spirit, a thought form, or a version of him that she created with her mind. She tells me that she worked with him, and he asked her to lunch one day. She just saw it as a friendly meal, but he had other intentions. She had somehow insulted him by tearing up something he had given her, and, in a fit of rage, he cut her throat with the glass from a jar. The guy wants to reenact it for me. I stop him, raising my hand, and I say, "No thanks." I ask him if he feels bad for killing her. He says, "No, I don't go there."

At this point, I call for a guide. It takes a couple of attempts. A woman shows up. I recognize her because she has shown up before in a couple of cases. Based on this familiarity, I assume she is assigned to me. She is interacting with both the woman and the man, and he gets angry and tackles her. She is surprised by his move and pushes him off, using her energy. I see his face, and it becomes hideously distorted for a moment. The guide says, "Well, that was unexpected." She then gets on to the business at hand. We are now in an outdoor setting with a mountain in the background. We are standing on a grassy area with a stream and a small walking bridge behind us. She tells the guy that the best she can do for him is a 64. A device with lights appears, and she says, "It looks like it jumped up to 77." She mentions some words that make me think of his payment or some responsibilities regarding his action, and that a higher number was going to mean that his responsibility had gone up. I took this at the time to mean his karmic responsibility. She leaves him there. Then the guide, the woman and I walk across the bridge. When I awake, I have complete memory of these events and I can recant them in full detail as if they have just transpired.

I went back to sleep and had a series of dreams and lucid dreams on the topic of murder. They were fascinating. One was where I was on the set of one of the CSI television shows, discussing with the creators that these shows probably aren't helpful. I told them it was like "murder porn." I remember one scene in which a man was standing outside a restaurant singing songs from the Sondheim musical, *Sweeney Todd*, a dark comedy about revenge and murder.

HELPING A FRIEND CROSS OVER

Some may be familiar with Tibetan dream yoga and its

HOW TO HAVE A GOOD LIFE AFTER YOU'RE DEAD

descriptions of the state known as "Bardo". In part, it entails the persistence of the illusion of life that can continue after physical death when a person goes into a dream state, not unlike our dreams every night. I have witnessed something like this before. Last night, I entered via an OBE into the dream reality created by a friend who passed away. Here's the story:

A friend of mine passed away yesterday afternoon at the age of 52. When I went to bed last night, I set my intention to go find him to make sure he was making the transition. Early this morning, I was having an OBE, and I found myself standing in front of a building. I was in an unfamiliar place, not in physical reality. I was outside the building when I heard his distinctive voice inside, so I went in. I followed his voice down some halls, and, sure enough, there he was, a big, strapping 20-something-year-old version of himself. At the time of his death, his disease had ravaged his body. I find people are usually their younger, vibrant selves.

He was obviously in a dream state and had created someplace he was familiar with. I greeted him, and he gave me a hug. I realized he didn't know he had died. I said, "Dave (not his real name, for privacy reasons), you do realize you just died." He replied, just as he always would when he would deny something he didn't think was true, "What? No, dude!" I repeated it and told him he died in the hospital. I told him to come with me, and I took him to a window in the building. I pulled him out the window and was flying with him. I said, "See, we are flying, and you can do this any time you want to." I was trying to find a light to take him to it but couldn't locate one. His energy wasn't high enough to allow us to remain flying and we landed in a grassy courtyard. I immediately made the request upon landing, "I would like one of Dave's guides." Immediately a video screen emerged out of the ground in front of us. A pleasant woman appeared and was smiling. I asked her to talk to Dave and help him understand that he had died. She tried, but he began to create other screens. After all, this was his Bardo dream world we were in, so he had control. As a sports enthusiast who liked to go to sports bars, he created a screen beside her with a football game on it. My guess is that this was his idea of mental escape. I tried to get him back on track, but I popped back into my body.

As I lay in bed afterward, thinking about what had just happened, it all made sense to me. He was a person with great powers of denial. He didn't think he was going to die, even as he wasted away and had to return to the hospital over the past two months. He was positive and upbeat that all was going to work out. On the days he felt better, he would go out of the house and even drive the car, which he wasn't supposed to be doing due to the medications he was taking.

I never know what will happen when a person crosses over. Some go directly through the portal, while others go into a dream state, as Dave obviously had. I will keep going back to check on him. I can find him through an intention if he hasn't gone through the portal and into the light. Maybe the guide was successful.

This situation is not uncommon, especially early on after the physical death. It can take a while as there is still some connection to the body and to this life. For some, it can take going to their own funeral to help them, or they wake up from the dream naturally. There is something like a gravitational tug that keeps pulling them toward moving on.

I write about these experiences to let people know what can happen when we die. For various reasons, not everyone goes directly through the portal and into the light.

DOCUMENTARY – THE LOWER FREQUENCY

Here's another case of getting confused about what can be done in the astral while I'm in it. I got stuck in the lower astral and decided to make the most of it. I made the rounds. It was like the Wild West in that anything and everything goes. These people were stuck in the dark regions of the afterlife, yet they figured out how to navigate it and set up a new life there. This experience went on for hours, and, at some point, I forgot the limitations of this reality. I came up with the idea of putting the memories of my time in this particular reality into a documentary. I had in my possession an iPad-like device and was recording everything I encountered using the video feature. The last scene was of a house, and musicians were playing outside. It was an instrumental country song with a thumping, driving melody. It reminded me of the band Fleetwood Mac's *The Chain*. It had that feel. The music is playing in my head as I am writing this. I was listening to a four-piece bluegrass-style band sitting on the porch of an old one-story house. The guy living in the house was notorious in this community. I wanted to make sure to record him for the documentary. I showed the uncut documentary to a group, and one of them told me that I must get the permission of all the people to use them in the documentary. I tried to think how I would go back to every situation I encountered during my stay there and get approval. Such is the delusion that can assert itself even in a lucid state on the astral plane. It would have been an incredible film.

NOTES: What I left this experience with, is that even though the settings of these lower astral frequencies are perpetually set in nighttime, and there are some rough characters there, they find a way to enjoy their lives and remain creative. I so wish I could show it to you or even explain what my night was like. Unfortunately, it would probably sound unremarkable. It was anything but, however. Just being there, seeing how these people lived and survived in this setting with its own rules and odd sense of ethics even though there were fights breaking out and all kinds of opportunity for mayhem, was absolutely fascinating.

I write this for my fellow explorers. Do not be afraid of these regions. There is much to be learned in all frequencies.

HOW TO HAVE A GOOD LIFE AFTER YOU'RE DEAD

RETREVAL OF SAMANTHA

I awoke around 2:15. The dog barked a couple of times downstairs. I got up to go down, but he stopped. I went back to bed, and in a hypnagogic state I recognized I could separate. I was having a bit of difficulty getting my legs to move. I was lying on my side, legs crossed at the shins, and I reached down and moved the second state version of my legs over the edge of the bed. As I stood up, I noticed my partner was also getting up. She was probably going down to check on the dog. I didn't know if she had really gotten up in the physical or was doing so in her second state. She walked by me in the darkness of the room and went out the bedroom door. I went downstairs to leave through the front door. When I got downstairs, it was dark; but I could see someone standing there. I took their arm, opened the door, and could see in the ambient light that it was a girl of about eleven or twelve. I asked her how she got here; she wasn't sure. I said, "come on, walk with me". We were walking down the street in what I assumed was our neighborhood. I asked her name; she said that it was Samantha. I wondered how long she had been in the house. I haven't exited through the front door in a couple of months.

I asked Samantha if she could see us, and she said yes. I said I hope we weren't too annoying. She replied, "Well, it's boring when you talk about politics." I laughed and said, "I can see how that could be." I then asked her if she knew she had died, and she replied with certainty that she had died. I asked her how, and she said that she was killed by a woman with blue streaks in her hair. I got a visual flash of the woman. I asked if she knew why she was killed, and she said that the woman thought she had taken something from her. I didn't press it. I inquired if she wanted me to help her move on to a happier location, and she said yes. I let her know that if I somehow disappeared from her view, she was to stay put and I would be right back. (I get concerned sometimes that I may blink out in the process.) I saw a streetlight up ahead, and I took her towards it. As we stood under the light, I said, "I need a guide to help Miss Samantha." In a matter of seconds, a doorway opened, and a woman stepped out. I asked her name, and she announced herself (can't remember her name.) She looked a bit sterner than I had hoped for, and I asked for a different guide, but she replied, "No, I'm it."

    I figured I would need to trust her but asked if I could come with them. She agreed, and we walked through the doorway and down a hall. We got to a series of rooms; it looked a bit like a medical clinic. There were some other guides there, and I asked them if they knew what I did. They acknowledged they did know. I asked if I could do this because they could see me better, and they said yes. I then asked how I was doing, and one told me that "extractions" had more than doubled since I had been in the area. I laughed and said, "Well, let's have a party!" and they found that amusing. I felt myself beginning to fade out, and I told them I was having an OBE and must go. I spun on one foot to take me to a different location and not lose state. I showed up in another place, which started a whole other episode of crazy.

GROUP RETRIEVAL – SOMETHING NEW LEARNED

I learned something new this morning. I woke up around 4 am, drank some water from a glass by the bed, and resumed my sleep. I quickly felt the awareness that I could get out. Nowadays, there is no vibration or a definitive sensation that prompts me to know I can roll out. Instead, it's a subtle knowing that my enteric body is "loose," and, if I want, I can advance the separation process. Some nights, getting free of the etheric state is easier than others. My ease of moving out seems to be related to the well-being of my physical body and my mental state. I ate six slices of pizza and two glasses of wine the night before and was nurturing a bad insect bite and taking some antibiotics for it. This combination, along with what is happening in the world right now, increased my difficulty in separation. I eventually succeeded after four or five attempts to move into my subtle body. I found myself in an outdoor setting that looked dark like the night. I ran into some people inhabiting this location. One tried to attach to me from behind, and I pulled him off and chastised him for his rudeness. I wasn't surprised to be in the lower astral, given my physical and mental state. I know how to get out of these places; the inhabitants often don't. Sometimes this is where my retrieval work starts, in the lower vibratory worlds. These are the folks who could most use the assistance that someone still in human has to offer. As I have mentioned in other writings, they can see those of us who are still in human realm and relate to our frequency more readily than if a helper were to appear there. The helpers might look partially transparent or completely invisible, just as they do in the physical world. Most of us don't see them, but they come if summoned.

I was surrounded by what I guess to be about fifteen of them. I informed them that I could get them out of this place if they wanted to come. I told them to follow me, and I looked around for a building with a light source. I have noticed that it can be no more illumination than what a single candle might put out, but any amount of light is helpful. I find it to be the only reliable indicator for places where I can exit. When I arrive at a light source, I look for stairs or, even better, elevators so I can move out of these locations by going upward. Some who travel can do it with their mind. I can spin on one foot and raise my frequency, but, in this situation, I had a group of people I was trying to lead. I had to conduct the operation using a protocol they would be familiar with. In this building, my only option was to move them through a series of doorways. I would take them through a door and down a short hallway and repeat until we reached somewhere with more light. At the end of the hallway, I called out that they must go through the door with me. As soon as we did, we were immediately in a lighter environment. The more illuminated the ambient environment, the higher the frequency. I knew I had more work ahead because there were no helpers to greet us. Also, everyone still looked the age they were when they had died.

As we walked to the next location, I start talking with a man named Paul. He was in a light brown sports coat, the cashmere style that used to be popular. I ask him if he minded telling me how he died. He wasn't sure. I started to lose my focus and found myself in a false awakening state in my bed; I began visualizing Paul so I could get back to the scene. Within moments, I was back walking with him. I do an exercise of rubbing my hands together to ground myself in the environment and I carry on with the job of getting these people to a higher frequency locale. We began picking up more people as we went, and I again used the same protocols. I now saw there were some stairs and doors.

I finally got them to a large room, and our group now had grown to thirty or more. Some still looked older and frail so I had to go higher still. One older man was there with his wife. He was dressed in his military uniform displaying some medals. I asked him about them. He said he fought in the Pacific and said a Japanese word; I assumed it was the island he was stationed on. I looked around for guides and spotted some. They came over and I considered my work done. I made a loud request for my group's attention and announced what an honor it was to have met them and to be a part of their journey. A couple of the helpers were smiling at me, and I got a little emotional.

As I left, I noticed a small group was still with me. Now I was no longer in the mode of retrieval. I was just making my way around a location in the astral that appeared earth-like and had a sea or ocean with a mountain cliff structure beside it. The illumination level looked a bit like sunset. There was a red and pink hue off on the horizon over the body of water. Beside the docks were boats, and there were restaurants and bars. I got caught up in the scenery, and I blinked out again. I overcame the urge to wake up in my bed. I focused on that setting so I could get back. It was successful, and I found the people who had followed me sitting in the restaurant/bar perfectly content, smiling. One had a cigarette. I was satisfied that this was as far as they wanted to go for now. They looked young and vibrant.

This is the point where I learned something new. I walked up some steps, and there was a balcony. I encountered someone I was a bit familiar with (I don't know her in this reality), and she asked me if I wanted to join her. I told her about what I just experienced with the group retrieval. She excused herself and said she would be back. I noticed a door that some people were carrying things through. It was on the level right below us. I asked her what that was. She said, "That is a place for people who pay." I didn't know what she meant, so I walked down the one flight of steps and opened the door. I immediately sensed it was the living area for people who desired to live in something like a retirement or assisted living situation. I saw a dining room and plates of food were being taken to the residents, but they were not all the same plates. Some of the meals looked better. I asked her about this discrepancy, and she explained to me something I hadn't heard before or even considered. She said that in this place, some people have more to spend than others based on the kindness and consideration they showed others in the life they lived. They have different accommodations and food reflecting this.

When I woke up around 7:30, I reflected on the oddness of the situation, which I encountered at the retirement home setting. First, I don't consider this to be how it works in all astral regions, but it seems that in this case, or at least in this community, there is such a thing as "kindness credits." These afford residents a more upscale afterlife experience. I find this fascinating. It reminded me of when I went to an exhibit for the *Titanic* and found out that a person's financial and social status altered their level of experience on the ship. This was evident down to the plates and flatware they were issued. They all got a boat experience that reflected their station in life. There may be a currency in the afterlife commensurate with one's frequency of consciousness. I am a foodie and like nice accommodations when I travel, so I do believe that from here on, I will seek to be kinder and more considerate out in the world.

MIKE MARABLE

MORRISON TELLS ME TO LIVE

After a series OBEs, I roll out around 4:30, and I am immediately greeted by a tall figure in my bedroom. It seems feminine. She says come with me and takes my hand, and we walk in the direction of our bathroom off the master bedroom, we enter a large room that is lit by a reddish glow, and there is a hall that doesn't exist in our home. She takes me to a small room that appears to be decorated to the taste of the occupant with a sitting area. She is this tall, beautiful black woman; he is also black. It appears to me that they have an androgenous mix of both male and female characteristics. He thanks her by name, which was not a name I have ever heard before. He introduces himself as Morrison. He asks me if I want to live. I say, "yes." He replies, "Good, you need to live." Then he leans over and whispers in my ear, "You need to live." I take this to mean that I should not waste my life. I tell him I feel that I am not doing much with it. He tells me, "We need you here to assist," and that beautiful things are happening because of what I and others are doing. I tell him that lately I feel that I have not been fulfilling my potential, and maybe I might just die; he said, "you..." He began to say "already" and stopped himself. I said, "I already did?" I was confused, so I asked, "When?" and was wondering if I was dead now. He said, "In 1961, it was in the kitchen, and you choked on something. It needed to happen." I have no recollection, and I asked if my mother was there. I got no answer. I blinked out, had a false awakening, and tried to go back by calling out his name. I wanted to finish the conversation with this guide named Morrison.

I went back to sleep after this experience. I then had a series of dreams about groups of men who would pray to God, and then go out and shout his name as they sought to find their runaway slaves. I was shown scene after scene of this: how slave owners sought God's help to find and hold onto their slaves. They even had a particular ceremony they would use and phrases they would cite.

RETREVAL – VISITING THE LIGHT

I woke at 3:01 a.m. and immediately went back to sleep. I had a series of amusing and interesting lucid dreams and OBEs. I partially awoke back in my bed and recognized the signs that if I wanted, I could rapidly breathe through my nose, raise my frequency, and have another OBE. I did this, and I soon separated.

I feel someone take my second state hand, and they pull me away from my body. I go with it to see what this is about. We are standing in the dark of a room with only the ambient light from the window, but I can tell it is a male. I take him outside, and it's a young man in his mid-20s, dark hair and dressed in contemporary clothes. (I never know how old the person is because, when we transition, we revert to the prime of life or a meaningful period in that life.) I ask him some questions, and he begins telling me about some mundane aspects of his life and where he worked. I ask him, "Do you think there is a chance you may have died?" He stops talking and thinks about it. He then remembers that, yes, he had died. I sometimes ask what happened but didn't want to take the time to learn more. I wanted to get him out of this earth-bound reality and to the light if I could.

I can tell a little about where I am in the astral by how dark it is. In the lowest reaches of the astral that I can go to, it's very dark, and if there are structures or thought forms, they are often illuminated by an amber hue. This space we were in was not that low but still had a nighttime sky. We were outside a house on a porch. It may have been his house, I don't know. I look up in the sky for a light. Often, the light will present like the moon above. Any light will do in this environment if it's above me. (A light above is an opening, I have found.) Normally, I will tell them to go to the light and show them they can fly to get there. Sometimes, I will fly them towards the light and tell them to continue the rest of the way. If I am not in a lower astral environment, as I was this time, I can take them to a "way station" and drop them off with helpers. This time, I felt the need to take him all the way to the light.

I had never done it this way before and had no idea what I might encounter. I take his hand, and we ascend upward toward the light. Flying is slower in the lower astral; we fly through the darkness, arrive at a platform and there is a light there. There is a wall and, for lack of a better word, a large button with some instructions. I push the button and a platform opens. There is an arch or gateway and a ramp down to where the two of us are standing. A woman walks down the ramp to greet us. I explain what is going on, and then two men show up. I repeat the story to them and explain that I do these rescues to help people continue their transition. They seem to understand. Then they take the young man up the ramp.

One of the men asks me to donate. My first instinct is a monetary donation. I reach into my astral body pocket and find two large coin-like objects. They look more like poker chips than coins; however, I hand them to him. He takes them and then asks me about these rescues that I do. I mention that I had done this for my father when he died. He asks my father's name, and I say, "Jim Marable." He then asks if I wanted to write his name on the board. I say sure, so he takes me over to the board. It is a large board, and I see something to write his name with. There are many names, and I see an open spot, so I write JIM MARABLE. I have never written anything in an OBE state before. In lucid dreams, it is very hard to write something and have it remain intact. What I write stays stable, and I am able to print it with very little trouble. I leave and tell him I may see him again. I then wake up in my bed. It's 7:05 a.m.

NOTES: As I lay in bed thinking about this unusual set of events, I was reminded of the ancient stories of crossing over the river Styx at death and needing to pay the ferryman to take one across. This is why bodies were buried with coins. Upon reflection, I think I could have probably donated anything. It seems to be more of a symbolic act, displaying gratitude for the assistance provided. We put so little effort into gratitude. Possibly, it helps the process along in non-physical realities. I have no idea why these circumstances arise; I just go with them.

These constructions of a reality with buildings, ramps, and boards to write names are possibly created to make the visitors feel more comfortable. But why make them push a button to gain entrance? Once again, I must admit that I do not understand the nature of the facades and why they exist.

HOW TO HAVE A GOOD LIFE AFTER YOU'RE DEAD

RETRIEVAL OF BART WITH GUIDES

Around 5:00 this morning, I had a conscious OBE that I entered via a lucid dream. I found myself in what I understood was a nursing home or hospital. I asked why I was here and waited for a response. A man wrapped himself around me, and I pulled him off. He was in a hospital gown. He was very old, bald, and must have worn dentures because all his teeth were missing. He was gaunt and thin. I used to call on nursing homes as a sales representative and owned a home health equipment company, so I know these facilities and the people who inhabit them, well.

I took the man outside and turned to look around at the building we just exited. The facility was connected to a church, and I asked him if he lived there. He said, "Yes." I asked him his name, and he replied, "Bart." I got some personal history from him; he told me he worked as a "lawyer." I then asked what kind of practice, and he said he worked for a gas company. I begin walking with him through a field, and the lighting appeared to be around dusk. The twilight appearance gave me some idea about what frequency we were in. This was one of the lower astral frequencies but not so low that I couldn't see a helper. I called out for a guide to assist as I was losing energy and didn't want to lose him. I heard voices coming toward me, and I recognized the signature energy of the individuals as guides. I handed him off and blinked out.

I gathered my energy and went back to find him by thinking

of his face and name. I was standing in a room, and he came up the stairs looking younger, wearing a nice suit and tie and was smiling at me. This made sense, as this is probably what he wore most days as a lawyer. He shared his gratitude. I told him I was glad I was able to help him. There were guides/helpers around going about their business. They were getting ready to meet and discuss something, and I asked if I could join them. I explained that I assist with retrieving people like Bart. They understood, and I asked them what they call this work, and the word I got from them was "extraction." I commented on the different garb each was wearing. I know from other conversations that they wear what is necessary to make the people they are helping feel more comfortable. I commented on this and their "costumes;" they found that humorous. One guide had on a military uniform, and he took off his hat. I jokingly asked if he was in the German Luftwaffe as it seemed to me to be what I might have expected a German WWII officer's uniform to look like. It was grey and formal. He just smiled. As I left them, it dawned on me that what he was wearing was a military uniform of either Ukraine or Russian Army. I am sure they have a lot of work to do there right now [2023]. I woke up around 7:00. I played back the details and grabbed my iPad to record.

HOW TO HAVE A GOOD LIFE AFTER YOU'RE DEAD

VISITING TWO CONSENSUS REALITIES

I spent what seemed like two Earth days in a couple of consensus realities. The first one started as a dream. I was invited to play golf by two individuals. I showed up for golf, and my deceased next-door neighbor, Dave, was there. Seeing him, I become lucid. I questioned if I am in a consensus reality. I helped Dave realize he had died after he passed in 2019. I figured that I had entered his consensus reality. He looked like a younger, healthier version of himself, not the sick person I had visited in the hospital as he died from a failing liver due to his alcohol consumption. I decided to check out his new life and agreed to play golf. I haven't golfed in a couple of years, but I am taking lessons currently. I was interested to see if my lessons helped my golf.

I had a false awakening and was successful in getting back to the place where we were to meet. I showed up at the clubhouse and found him talking with the two who would be going out with us. It looked like early morning; he introduced me to a doctor friend of his and another person. They were already drinking. They were about to head to the first tee. I told them I would meet them there. I wanted to look around the clubhouse. It was well-appointed with equipment and apparel. I figured it was time to follow them, and I looked around the shop for some clubs to use. I won't go into detail, but it I found out that it's difficult for non-residents of this consensus reality to navigate this area well enough to play golf.

They fully believe it is real, and because I don't see it that way, it is not as stable for me. I decided to abandon the golf idea.

My friend obviously wanted to continue the things he enjoyed in life, including drinking. I wondered if this was a place for people with similar addictions or preferences. Maybe I was drawn to this locale because I enjoy golf and a drink, too. I like a glass of wine with dinner. Would this be enough to allow me into this reality?

I asked for an "addiction counselor." I know in these realms that whenever you ask for assistance, someone always shows up. After what seemed like 30 seconds, a hallway appeared, and I walked down it. At the end, I saw a woman leaning out of a booth. I told her my name and asked her what my addiction was. She looked down at something and said, "Advancement." I laughed and thanked her. Walking away, I thought, that's not really an addiction. As I write this, I am considering that it could possibly be an addiction, if it were to consume someone's life. I started to ponder this idea, and I woke up.

I lay there, going back over this experience in my mind, and I fell back to sleep. This time, I found myself in another consensus reality. I learned that this was answering my questions. It was confirming for me that the previous experience was indeed a consensus reality. In this new one, I seemed to spend a day and a half within a community getting to know some of the residents very

HOW TO HAVE A GOOD LIFE AFTER YOU'RE DEAD

well, and I had considerable time to ask them questions about their life there. I could write a book just on this experience. Since many of the details might be mundane for a reader, I will keep it brief. Their lives were unremarkable, which is sort of the theme of the experience in general. Here are some impressions that may help in understanding what these places are like. I had never stayed so long in one of them before. I originally assumed that what I was seeing was just part of a larger place. I learned from this visit that some of these realities were small and confined. This reality had a lake and a town with restaurants and gathering places, and yet that made up the totality of their space. It reminded me of the town in the movie *The Truman Show* or one of the settings for a *Hallmark Channel* town featured in the television series. If you have seen the movie, the main character Truman and the residents don't desire to leave their town. They are lost in their routines and are content staying there. I find this is the same attitude among the residents of this locale. The people were very congenial, and everyone I talked to knew they had died. They had taken up the familiar routines that they had on earth. It felt like a retirement community.

I got to know one of the residents; her name was Tutti. I asked her how she died. She said that she went into tachycardia after eating some sugary gum. I inquired if she had been a diabetic, and she said yes. She told me of the incident, and she said it happened "last night." I reminded her that she had been here awhile. This jogged her memory, and she remembered she had been there "five" (she used a term that seemed related to time that I am not familiar with.) She had a home there, a small apartment. She had a book on the table. I picked it up and looked at it. It seemed to be a picture book of aspirations that she had during her life. It contained idealized pictures of her. It then came to life in an animated way in my mind in a way that could not be revealed in pictures and text alone. I could also understand what they represented. She had wanted to open a bakeshop and a store that sold high-end home furnishings and bedding such as comforters, sheets, and furniture for the bedroom. She wanted romance in her life and wanted to look glamorous. The photography in the book was exceptional, as if she had hired a professional to make this book up for her. I saw how her shop would look, and it was tastefully done. I asked her if she ever thought about leaving this reality to "upgrade?" She didn't seem to have ever considered that. I asked her questions like, "Do they have animals there?" and she said no. I have seen dogs in other consensus realities, but not in this one; but that doesn't mean they weren't there.

At the end of my stay in this town, there was a gathering of a small group of people, most of whom I had met during my visit. They had food and drinks. I sensed it was something they did routinely. I thanked them for their hospitality. They knew I hadn't died and was just visiting. (This was established in earlier conversations I had with them.) Some wanted me to know that they were evolving during their time there, and one joked that he changed what he was doing based on something we had talked about. Then I woke up.

IMPRESSION: I have spent enough time in these consensus realities to compare them. I always get the sense that I am just visiting a portion of the available setting. Maybe there are much larger ones, but whatever the size, they aren't endless, and the residents seem a bit confined there. Why that is, I don't know. Then I considered that in our human reality, we pretty much do the same thing with our routines. We travel to the same places using the same routes and generally interact with the same people throughout our lives. We may move sometimes, but we usually take our routines with us and start them over again in the new location. Many of us live our lives in a confined way. We have created the illusion of more variety than we have. It's a lot to think about.

RETRIEVAL OF ADAM

I conducted a retrieval of a man, and when I asked him if he wanted to go to the light, he said he did. As I walked him down the dark street, I saw a light up ahead. I began asking him questions. He said his name was Adam and he was from Tennessee. I asked what town and he said, "Memphis". Since I have been to Memphis, I asked if he had ever been to the famous rib joint, *Rendezvous*. He said, "Absolutely." We reached a corner lit by a single streetlight, and there were other people there. I asked for a guide for Adam and saw a man who I thought might be a guide, but he wasn't. I then saw a woman dressed in canary yellow with some sort of tall hat. She noticed us, and I walked in her direction. When I reached her, I asked, "Are you his guide?" She confirmed that she was and was smiling at both of us, so I said, "I would like to introduce you to Adam." She greeted him, then looked at me and said, "I knew you before you started doing this." I blinked out before I could get more information about what she meant.

NOTES: Straightforward retrieval. I don't know or have never known anyone personally named Adam. I have no recollection of this woman either.

HISTORY OF THE AFTERLIFE

I woke up at 3:20 and went to the bathroom. I remain awake for what I estimate to be an hour. I get the subtle cues that I can roll out. I do so and go through the doors of our bedroom and see the living room below. I float down and go out through the front door. Things seem a bit foggy, so I say, "more clarity" and "more energy." This propels me into another scene and an interesting adventure which lasted until 9:00 this morning. I could write ten pages on the events that came out of these experiences, but I will just go over some of the unusual aspects that got my attention.

I must have been hungry because in the first room a man

HOW TO HAVE A GOOD LIFE AFTER YOU'RE DEAD

brings in a tray with many kinds of Sushi. I sit down at a low Japanese table to sample some of it. It is a beautifully created artistic arrangement of food, so I sample some of them. There are sauces that I have never seen before. I try one of the bites that look like salmon. It tastes different from any sushi I have had: not bad, just different. I move out of that room and find myself in a scene at an upscale bar. I look down, and I am wearing a suit.

I am not sure why I am there, but having on a suit tells me that I have flipped into an alternative reality timeline. A woman comes up to me. I don't recognize her, and she says, "There you are. I was looking for you. We won the case." I asked, "The law case. I won the case?" She replies, "Not just you; the team." I get the feeling we are romantically involved based on the way she is talking to me. I look in a reflective glass, and it's not me. I am shorter and have dark hair. In this reality, I have entered a character who is a lawyer. This goes on for a while, so I will move to the most interesting thing that happened in this part of the adventure. The alternative personality situations usually turn out to be very interesting.

I leave and walk around through some corridors, and I see a guy walking behind me. This is common; I call them guides, so I stop and chat with him. I ask his name, and it's David. I tell him that I am a traveler in this reality, and I am completely aware of the circumstance. He says, "That is impossible. I wouldn't be here if that's the case!" (I took it to mean that I am still alive.) I ask him to take me to another world so I can see the beings there. He then goes over and opens a panel in the wall, and we walk in a room where there are people sitting around. They don't look unusual, but they all have something like a small pearl-like ball on the top portion of their ears. I ask about it, and one of them asks me if I want one. I say, "Sure; will it hurt?" The person I am talking to says no, and then places it on the upper part of the inside of my ear along the rim. He then steps back and fires a beam from a handheld rod. The people there seem delighted that I have joined them. For some reason, I don't ask them what it is. I guess I'll find out.

I ask David to take me back with him, and he drops me off at what I come to understand is a dispatching station for these guides. I tell them my story, and they are equally surprised that I am there. I ask if any of them want to work with me on a regular basis. Most raise their hand. I ask the head guy if I can work with David since I got to know him. He agrees. I ask them what they are called or how should I refer to them. He says that they refer to themselves as "singers." We finalize the arrangement, and he says something along the lines that this is an interesting "booking" for David. The next time I get out, I will ask for David.

The final thing I do before I leave is to ask to be shown the history of the afterlife. Immediately, a sloped shelf opens out of nowhere, and a wallet-sized, black, smooth, rounded object slides down right in front of me. In the left-hand bottom corner, I see four numbers and a red square button. I knew if I pushed that button, I would be taken to another reality stream. I wasn't ready to do that for some reason. My sense is that this may be an adventure that should be its own thing, and I had been lucid for a long time. I didn't want to blink out during something important. When I go to investigate the history of the afterlife, I want to have a detailed plan.

RETRIEVAL OF UMA JEAN

I had a rather routine retrieval last night. Her name is Uma Jean, and she is from Indiana. She says she got stuck here because of some "asshole." I ask her twice if she wants to move out of this realm. (She was earthbound). She confirms she is ready. I tell her we need to look for a light source and we find one quickly. I call for a guide, and, almost before I get the words out, a rather androgynous person steps up and introduces himself to her as Uma Jean's guide. I stick around and talk to the guide who came for her. There are several people walking around, socializing, and I ask him, "Are all these people who died?" and he says no, some were just out doing things in their dreams. I ask what percentage have died. He scans the area and says about half. I say, "So, living people and the dead talk to each other?" He says that they can. He then says, "I have a message for you." He pulls out what looked like a paper, and there is some writing on it. It is from a person named Phil that I had done a retrieval for a long time ago. Phil said he made it just fine and thanked me for my help. It's the first time I have ever gotten word back from someone I helped. I am moved and happy he is ok.

The guide asks me if I had done the "impressions" for the Uma Jean. I take it to mean that this is something that is done for the person as part of the process, but I don't know what those entail. I tell him I don't know how to do these but was willing to learn. I then blink out.

I had more OBEs throughout the night, as is often the case after the first one. I met another traveler. I don't know how I knew who she was but had seen her somewhere. I asked her where she was from, and she said a place I had never heard of. I can't remember the name. I said, "I have never been there." She replied with a humorous kind of directness, almost like sarcasm, "Then get a ticket." I asked her more questions, and each one was answered in the same short, pithy reply that was both funny to me and a bit dismissive. It was completely telepathic, as are all these conversations. I got the feeling that she was not from an earth dimension since no one here that I have ever encountered communicates in this style.

VISIT TO A TRANSITION WAY STATION

I wake at 2:14 and go back to sleep in what I estimate to be about twenty minutes. I immediately have an OBE. I hang around close to earth this time and float around, examining the tops of trees. We never get to see these, so I thought I'd check them out. I then look at the details on the roofs of houses and buildings. It's what you expect for the most part, other than there were berries and moss on the top of trees that I didn't expect and some broken tiles on the roofs and twigs that had blown up there from the trees. One house has some solar panels. They have a slight film of dirt on them. I come back and go out again and this time I float up through the ceiling of a house, and I am in a large attic. It is the kind of attic that could be found in old houses with slanted eaves conforming to the roofline. There is a woman there, and she appears to be middle-aged. I ask her if she is a guide, and she says no. I ask to meet my guide, and she points to a woman sitting on a trunk. It is an older black woman with white hair. She smiles at me with this wonderful smile, and I tell her how beautiful she is. I ask her some questions about what she does as a guide. She explains that she helps us make choices that might protect us and what we came to do. I fade out before I can ask her more questions or her name. I try to go back there but am not successful.

The last experience is the most interesting. I am in a building, and it is segregated off by living conditions. I figure out that the people who are there are poor or lived a more modest existence on Earth. I recognize this as temporary living quarters for people who died. I have visited others, but this one is different in that the conditions are quite bare and unattractive. I wonder if this is how they will have to live out their post-transition lives.

Then I get, for lack of a better word, paged to come to

administration. I hear my full name announced. I show up and say, "I am Mike, I was paged". A woman says, "Yes I, that was me." She seems to indicate that I was doing something as a visitor there that they preferred I not do. (I understood at the time what that was but didn't when I woke up). I take the opportunity to ask some questions. I ask why the people are divided like this into different living conditions. It is explained to me that they selected these environments based on their expectations. I wasn't sure if this meant it was provided for them or if the residents created it this way themselves. I make the comment that people can adapt to better circumstances. They laugh at my comment. I then protest a bit, and one of the people in charge explains that they were only there for the equivalent of two human years, then they were "Free to go wherever they want". I ask if they were given any guidance about where to go next but don't get a clear answer. I then ask, "Do most go back into the human earth experience?" And she answers, "no". I am a bit surprised by this. I wake up at 6:44. I had been out there a long time, it seems.

I am continually surprised by what I learn on the "other side". Also, it has been my experience that the guides I meet, when I help people cross over, don't volunteer a lot of information but will answer questions. They won't go into detail if it's not important to my role, it seems. It appears I am on a need-to-know arrangement with the guides. It is possible that they get a variety of visitors and have identified me as a particular kind of visitor who

HOW TO HAVE A GOOD LIFE AFTER YOU'RE DEAD

is not a dreamer or someone who is getting ready to transition. My feeling is that they tolerate me. Their manner is businesslike. My impression is that they take their work seriously and are focused on what needs to be done.

A NEW FRIEND ON THE OTHER SIDE

I wake up in my second state. I am immediately confronted by a young man. I ask him the routine questions to see if he understands that he has died, and I escort him out of my house. I have started adding questions, such as why they come to me. This often gets some interesting replies.

The second person I meet is a woman whose name is Lily. I ask her why she came to me, and she says that she didn't know what else to do. It's gotten to the point where about half of the of time I get out, I am conducting retrievals. I don't mind, but I'd like to do something else sometimes. Of course, I can't just leave them. This takes me to the next part of the story.

After the third retrieval, I decide to go to what I call "customer service." If I ask for a guide, I have noticed that on occasion, I will end up in a room with guides and often they look like ordinary people. When I talk with them, it isn't much different than talking to any person. They always look busy and focused on their task, so the conversations are brief and to the point. Sometimes, when I deliver someone to these places, I ask questions. On one occasion, I was told by a guide that they are available to help us humans and can reach us in dreams. If someone helps you in a dream, it could be a guide. We are required to make a request for assistance, however, to receive it. We would need to remember the dream and act on the information we receive.

I ask for some information during this visit. I want to see if someone can help me slow this down. I wonder if something about me is attracting these discarnate individuals. I want a method to shut it down when I want to.

My sense is that this isn't what these guides do, so I ask one of them if they can connect me with an "angel." To me, an angel is not a religious figure; it's a name for those who have abilities that guides don't possess. They agree to help me and honor my request. I fade out of this scene, wake up in my second body in bed, and I go into a dream. Almost immediately, a woman shows up who looks to be in her 30's with dark hair. I know she is in the class of beings that I had requested. I tell her what is going on, and she listens patiently. She directs me to sit down, comes over me, and starts examining me by moving her hand in a hovering motion around my body. I ask her name, and she replies, "Niya." She asks me if I have always had this sensitivity. I am not sure what she is referring to. She acknowledges that I need some "repairs" and places her hands around the back of my head and neck. I then feel a pleasurable jolt of energy come into my body. It is strong enough that it makes my back arch. It is very pleasant but intense. I find myself very taken with her. I want to know more. I ask her if they have music in her world. She says yes, and I ask if I can hear her favorite song. Immediately, beautiful music surrounds us, like nothing I have ever heard. I try to discern a particular instrument, but I can't identify one.

I fade back into my second body in my bed and enter a lucid experience. Now I am walking up some stairs, and I feel invisible fingers pulling on my thumb. It stops for a moment, then starts again, and I go with it, letting this invisible person guide me up the stairs. I am standing in front of a door. I open it, and there stands Niya. She says that she contacted me because she wants to work with me again because I am "wired" uniquely. She says she will be available to me if I want to request her specifically. My sense is that because we have free will, I need to make such a request.

I wake up very excited. It appears I have a new friend to work with. I can't wait to see where this goes. I told my partner this morning. She said she knew something was going on because I was talking during my sleep.

MIKE MARABLE

A WARNING IN ENGLAND

I was vacationing in England with my partner and staying in a 700-year-old manor house once owned by Henry VIII. I planned to have an OBE to see what I might uncover in a property with this much interesting history. I was successful, and it was not at all what I expected but much more than I anticipated.

I got out, it was dark, and I went out the door into a dark hallway of the building we were staying in, which was previously the stables for the main manor. I followed the hall and found some steps and took them down. At the bottom of the steps, it turned into a structure that looked like an underground tunnel. There were people walking around in the dark. I knew intuitively they were discarnate.

Some started to follow me. A woman grabbed my arm; she seemed distraught. It wasn't getting any lighter, so it dawned on me on me to yell, "Look for the light!". After I did this, I saw a flicker of light, as if it might be a single candle about fifty yards in front of us. I went towards it and walked into an old village with cobblestone streets. It was lit in that amber light, which I am familiar with, that presents in the lower astral environments. The sky above was pitch black. It was like a movie set housed in a black void. My thought at the time is that this is probably a façade constructed by guides, a collection point or waystation. I looked around; there were now about fifty to seventy people behind me.

HOW TO HAVE A GOOD LIFE AFTER YOU'RE DEAD

We turned the corner, and there was a slight incline of the street. There were guides there directing people up the street towards a light now as wide as the street. A man came up to me who looked to be in his early thirties, around six foot, and addressed me by name. I recognized him but couldn't recall his name. He was someone I was acquainted with back in Richmond, Virginia, back in the 1970s. I met him at a nightspot all of us went to back then. I greeted him. He said, "You are alive; I want to tell you something." I told him I am just visiting. He continued, "I want to tell you about something happening; there are five hundred people in a group gathering up guns, and they are going to kill; it will be a massive killing of a bunch of people. You need to tell someone."

I got the sense it was in North America. I regret that I didn't ask the appropriate questions of where and when. I did ask if it was set in the future timeline and if it could it be averted, and he affirmed it could. I said that I wouldn't know how to get to some agency and explain this. Can you imagine if I put in a tip into the FBI and then had to explain how I came upon this information? I said, "I'm sorry, I can't remember your name". He said, "Jeff McAlester." I remembered he used to hang out with a guy named Bob back then. I mentioned this, and he pulled out a device the size of a cell phone and presented a picture of Bob. I recognized him. The two of them had bought a business, a high-end butcher shop. Jeff had sliced off half his finger early on, and a surgeon reattached it. He was about five years older than me back then.

I inquired about his life afterwards because I lost track of him. He said he stayed single and was successful. I asked him how he likes being dead. He replied it isn't much different. Finally, I asked a question I have never thought of before for some reason, "How did you know I wasn't dead?" He replied, "Because you have some blue stuff around you", and he pointed to my head. I found this interesting and turned around to walk back down the street towards the direction I came. The street was now empty. I decided to just return to my bed, closed my eyes and willed myself back. I was so stable in the OBE it took a bit of effort. I could have stayed longer if I had wanted to, but I wanted to make sure not to lose any details. It felt important to remember the information I was given.

TRIPLE RETREIVAL

Someone mentioned to me that a person named Bruce Moen also attended the Lifeline program at the Monroe Institute and conducted retrievals. It turned out that he wrote three books on his experiences. I ordered his book, *Afterlife Knowledge Guidebook*, and used some tips that he offered in his book, this morning when I conducted a retrieval.

This one started with removing an attachment. I picked up a "hitchhiker" while traveling. My sense is that it took place when I traveled in a non-lucid state. I can sometimes tell when I have one

HOW TO HAVE A GOOD LIFE AFTER YOU'RE DEAD

because there is a heaviness on my back and shoulders during the day, and I get dream material that doesn't fit. I have been working with my dreams for many years and know when something is amiss. I can also sense their mood. If I believe I have one, I try to get them to leave by talking to them and providing instructions. This one didn't want to go. When I rolled out this morning, I raised my energy level and pulled him off me. I took him outside through the bedroom window. As we moved outside, he asked, "Who are you?" I told him my name. I asked his, and he said, "William".

This guy did not believe he was dead and did not want to leave. I decided to take him to a service location for pick up. I delivered him to a male guide. I asked the guide how I was doing here. The guide said I was doing well and offered a suggestion, which I tried later.

I then entered another frequency level. I know this because the first location was in a level that looked like one that we might mistake for our physical world. I was now in a brighter area; a woman arrived with another man, and they heard me talking about someone having died. They wanted to know what was going on. The woman was upset. She suddenly realized that she died and now doesn't know where to go. I gave her a hug, and the man with her, who was very tall, said he was in a hospital. He said he didn't feel as if he had died. I explained that he wouldn't have felt anything when he died; he would have just nodded off, like when you go to sleep.

I talked with them, and they now understood that they had died and seem ok with it. I called for a guide to help them immediately before I blinked out. I did my best and hope they figured out where to go.

I sometimes gain additional knowledge during the retrieval that I didn't have before. For example, one time I was shown what happens when someone kills a person. It seems that there is some sort of penance or service that gets added to that soul consistent with the amount of life expectancy left for the person they killed in that life. It is expected that you do something for that length of time in the next incarnation, possibly to be of service. I can't know exactly what the compensation would look like. In one scenario, I was shown a man who killed someone. The person he killed was a criminal who would have been arrested for another crime. It was explained to me that he would have been killed in prison after two years. This means the compensation period would only be two years earth time for killing that person.

RETRIEVAL OF GRETCHEN

I woke around 2:30 this morning, and as I entered the state before sleep, I realized I could detach. There is a figure standing in the room. It looks like a woman. It is dark and I take her over to the window so I can see her face in the ambient light from outside.

I ask if she knows she died, and she says yes. I move her

out through the window and onto the ground below. I ask her if she is ready to move on to somewhere more pleasant, and she agrees to let me help her. I usually ask this unless I forget. I want to see if they are open to the idea, and it seems like the polite thing to do. I ask her name, and she tells me her name is Gretchen. I ask when she died, and she replies very specifically, "Two days ago." (I can't rely on the accuracy of this as the sense of time may be impacted by the dimensional change and other factors). I ask how it happened. She says something hit the house but doesn't elaborate.

    I walk her in the direction of the corner of our house, asking for a guide and help for Gretchen. It remains dark, and I realize we are earthbound because none appears. Either they can't reach us, or I couldn't see them. I needed to get her to higher ground, so to speak. I need to find some light source to move towards. I see a light behind our yard and a fireworks display off in the distance. Maybe she likes fireworks, I think to myself, and this will make her feel more comfortable. We cross a ravine and go over a bridge. Gretchen is coming out of her lethargy; she looks less pale and is getting chattier. I ask her more questions and start with inquiring as to her last name. She tells me, and I ask her to spell it. She does and then volunteers her home address and even her parents' names without prompting. I can't remember this information and have already forgotten how she spelled her name. I ask her to spell it again, and she chides me, "I did. Are you going to remember it this time?"

I have trouble remembering some specifics like a series of numbers or distinct facts unless there is something I can anchor them to that has relevance. If there are more than two syllables and it's not a common word, then I have difficulty bringing the memory back with me.

We are approaching a lighted area. This seems to stir something in her. She is now wearing a pretty dress, and her face and hair look younger. She now seems as if she is ready to go. Somehow, she knows what to do. She floats in the air and takes off like a rocket into the semi-lit sky. After she reaches a height that looks like hundreds of feet up, a light appears with some colors. I see her interacting with it. I feel comfortable that she will be ok.

The light then pulls her inside, and she becomes enmeshed with it. It appears complete. I can see her on the other side, and I smile and wave at her.

My job is done, so I start walking back. I forget that I don't need to do this, but, as I walk down a path, I notice a black dog is with me. I pet my little spirit helper and head home.

NOTE: This is the second time I have seen someone float off and move rapidly though a portal like this. The first time was with my father.

HOW TO HAVE A GOOD LIFE AFTER YOU'RE DEAD

LOST AND FOUND RETREVAL

A young man aged nine, according to him, followed me back home. I got up about 2:00, went to the bathroom, immediately fell back into a hypnagogic state and noticed the subtle signs that I could separate. There he was, a shadow in the room, not enough life force to have even the slightest illumination. I approached him and saw it was a child. I asked if he knew he had died; he said he didn't. He was surprised and then upset to learn that he had. I went through my usual process of taking him downstairs and comforting him with words of caring encouragement. I felt that my state wasn't strong but I was trying to comfort him. He was pulling on my own life force, and I didn't have the reserve necessary, it seems, so I blinked out. I had lost a retrieval. I semi awoke but fought hard to regain state so I could go look for him. This began a night-long search. I hadn't gotten a name but remembered his face, and I used this image to see if I could find him. I couldn't let the little guy wander around in the lower frequencies without assistance.

As I set my intention, I showed up in a middle-frequency level, and someone had left clues for me on a bulletin board beside the road. It gave me a history on him, what had happened, along with his name. I then found myself in a room with adults supervising some children, and I asked if they knew him. One of them gave me the name of the place they saw him last, which I used to help me find him. This sleuthing went on like this for a while until I found him. I am surprised that I did, frankly. I took him with me, and I saw we are in the lower astral. I looked around and noticed we were being followed by a large man, dressed in dark clothing, and a Dobermann Pinscher. The dog approached us, snarling. I assumed this was a manifestation of the boy's fears, and I was not concerned; I kept moving him toward a light where I found help for him. I woke up at 6:58 am., relieved that I had found him.

NOTE: This is maybe one of the reasons why more people are not able to conduct retrievals. It takes a lot of practice and sometimes considerable effort to hold state. I usually can hold, but it seems his fear and need of my life force energy drained me quickly. This happens occasionally, and I am usually able to go right back. This time, I had difficulty finding the person. I won't conjecture on why. Not having a name might have had something to do with it. The material left on a public bulletin board on the street was a fascinating addition to the experience and something to keep in mind. We always have help.

The Earth Experience Is a Hot Ticket

When we take on the human form, we forget that the restless energy that animates us is eternal. We believe ourselves only to be this form, and that this is the true reality. The personality construction that we utilize to navigate around in this world is a critical part of the Earth experience. There are some philosophies that propose the part of us we most identify with, the ego self, as it is often called, is responsible for our suffering and is something to be overcome. A variety of disciplines are prescribed for loosening its grip on our psyches. For some, it may be part of their learning curriculum to loosen the ego or even try to escape and live in a self-realized state. Others choose a fully immersive experience into the human and the full adoption of the personality self provides the best opportunity for learning. Not remembering the true nature of our being is part of the attraction of entering into the human. It can be said that it's a feature, not a bug, for an optimal Earth incarnation. There is no right or wrong way to have the human experience, though there are institutions that try to promote and impose the idea that there is. There is no failure per se; it is all simply experience.

For example, there is rigid dogma in established religion around ideals like morality, and these can elicit judgements. These are illusory constructions created by society. There is no universal form of judgment. There *are* judgments that we impose on ourselves, and others may join in, but these belong to the personality. We maintain feelings of separation during the human incarnation, and this allows for an individualized sense of self. Of course, the animating energy within "all that is"—what we think of as universal consciousness—accepts everything as itself. Nothing separates you from the source except the illusion of such. This illusory experience is not a flaw in the design: it is essential in maintaining the intense learning environment that is available on this planet. You might be surprised to learn that it is a hot ticket and honor to be able to come here. This is due in part to the unique opportunity for accelerated evolution that is possible within an environment where our true nature and underlying reality are veiled from our awareness. Think of it as like going to a supercharged theme park like the one in the *HBO* series *West World,* where an alternative reality is constructed for the visitors to play out their fantasies in a safe environment, all the while knowing they are just visiting a temporary world and can go back home at any time. They understand it's not real, and they aren't really the characters they are playing.

The physical earth frequency concept is similar to this, except that when you enter this park, all memory is removed of our full self, and we believe we are that character and the physical appearance of the environment is "real." This makes for an intense and instructional experience.

It is highly sought out by adventurous beings in other dimensions of reality who are willing to take the chance they will get caught up in cause-and-effect circumstances that may necessitate a return. This possibility is worth the risk for many it seems.

The opportunity to learn is enhanced by this illusion of one's own mortality. We find it difficult to grasp why anyone would go through this from our earthbound perspective. After you leave the human form it will make perfect sense, however. That we identify with the physical body and buy into the belief that it can die amps up the emotional charge; it takes courage to enter the human experience.

There are many millions of beings who are here now and have come into the human experience to assist and be part of a critical time in Earth's evolution. They are now, and what we think of as the past, actively assisting in an active transformation of the frequency on this planet. Graduation to a higher vibrational state is part of the evolution of planets in the physical universe. It is a major event in the life of a planet. I am happy to report that ours successfully made it, though it was touch and go there for a while. It required the assistance of many, many beings: those who volunteered to incarnate and help raise the frequency. You may know some or be one yourself and not realize it. Others did their part outside of this frequency. The result of these efforts led to an important breakthrough for Earth. Much effort has been taken to "activate" a portion of the memory of as many as possible to maximize their energy and raise the frequency here. Some were able to fully open to their memories. Others intuitively understood they were here for a purpose greater than themselves and chose life paths of service to others. Some got caught up in the illusion and emotional gravity of this reality construction. All who volunteered to incarnate into a human body for this transition did so with the full understanding that they might not be able to fulfill their mission. The risk that they could get caught up in the energetic gravity of cause and effect was very real. That original intention of service to others and help facilitate a higher frequency thought form for Earth still worked even if activation didn't occur.

Now I realize that this will sound like complete nonsense to some readers. I debated even putting this in the book because, frankly, it's a bit much to digest. I accept this and understand, I really do. For those who are skeptical, I ask that you give me the benefit of the doubt or possibly read it like a nice story coming from a person with good intentions.

HOW TO HAVE A GOOD LIFE AFTER YOU'RE DEAD

YOUR EARTH EXPERIENCE HEADSET

The human brain participates as part of a larger system while we are alive in the physical three-dimensional reality stream. The brain's default mode network, as identified by neuroscience, serves to maintain the executive functions. This part of our earth headset, the brain, maintains the illusion of separation from the surrounding environment and provides a sense of linear time. It is partially responsible for the sense of an individualized self, the ego, if you will. This is your localized storage and operation system. There is also a non-local "cloud server" which could be called the mind. It has more features. These systems share access to relevant consciousness elements for this life. People who have NDEs and have no break in the continuity of their conscious awareness have switched to a non-local server, at least in part, to maintain the sense of self and memories of the most current life. Though it appears that the brain is not functioning biologically, all the atoms and particles that it is constructed from continue to retain information at the quantum level. Information is never lost. That this is not yet recognized by science is consistent with the materialist philosophy that medicine relies upon. It continues to exchange information even though there is a "dead" brain. Every pulse of thought, emotion and action creates a record that is uploaded in the larger consciousness field, where it remains as a holographic record, capturing forever all information and emotional content of that person throughout the physical life just lived and all others.

The brain is perfectly designed to accommodate the basic needs of survival for the Earth Experience. It filters out far more than it takes in. You see mostly the world that you need to see.

If someone wants to gather information beyond the basic program, this is available in altered states like dreams. Breakthroughs can also happen through the use of meditation and psychedelics in larger doses; these can intercede by taking the brain's executive functioning guardrails offline temporarily. Interrupting the brain's default mode network gives it the freedom to explore outside of its normal constraints and creates alternative connections. You have abilities and knowledge of which you are unaware.

One can meditate hours each day for years and yet remain oblivious to other realities. These practices do assist us to gain more insight into our own natures and train the mind and brain to be more flexible and less locked into physical reality. You were meant to be here; you chose this more limited experience even if you don't remember.

We have a signature frequency attached to consciousness. It is our passport to access other dimensions. If you want to impact your evolution and gain a fast-track pass, it is best obtained through empathy, compassion, service, and love. Just the desire to be of service can mean more than the act of service itself. It's really the intention, not necessarily the action, that has the most impact on the energetic field.

Acquiring knowledge is a worthy pursuit, yet it is the development of skills with the purpose of benefitting the whole that seems to be the most impactful contribution one can make. These skills are never lost and are essential during your current lifetime and after. We never go backwards, though we can temporarily regress. Choosing to make this the default way of being is *the* noble pursuit recognized in all dimensions of reality. If one can accomplish this within the cloaked state that exists in the Earth learning environment, that earns a standing ovation around the universe. You will understand this better after you "graduate" from this lifetime.

REINCARNATION FACT AND FICTION

Let's just get the debate settled straight away on this topic. Reincarnation is a real thing. It doesn't matter what you think about it or even that you consider it to be true within your belief system or world view. We must live in this version for now. It's not important that you consider reincarnation in your daily life or even know about. You could be completely oblivious to it in the grand scheme of things because it's all about this slice, this piece of our expansive self's download into the reality stream you think of as your life. The one you are consciously aware of right here, right now. Reincarnation is an interesting topic to think about, yet we can't fathom how it unfolds throughout the larger reality system. I am not aware of any research, studies or books about reincarnation that have been able to include an explanation that incorporates a multidimensional, non-linear gestalt. Sequential time as we experience it is illusory. Science even embraces this now. In this dimension we see a progression of incarnations within a linear time perspective. This is how our mental equipment processes the idea of reincarnation. We experience the past as no longer existing. However, it does and it's dynamic.

This is not a slight against human intelligence or ingenuity. We are like those fish I talked about in an earlier section. It is always going to be difficult for beings living in a three-dimensional reality system to relate to the notion of the absence of linear time. Once someone is outside of the human sandbox it gets easier. People who say, "I don't want to reincarnate," will be surprised to learn that, in some dimensions you already have. You enjoy concurrent existences. I will cover this in detail in a "future" book.

Reincarnation is an interesting subject to contemplate and even romanticize about.

We wonder what interesting lives we might have had in the past. Our knowledge of human history comes mostly from movies and books. These fictionalized depictions inspired by our desire for the romance are populated with historically famous people, adventure, and glamorous notions of royalty. Most folks living on earth throughout human history lived simple, brutal lives in harsh times, mired in poverty and ruled over by brutal overlords. Famine, plagues, and squalor most likely dominated your daily life. It was not particularly romantic.

It is an important consideration to remember that our beliefs and state of mind, after we die, influence our experiences. These are more malleable thought-responsive environments. I would like to comment on some discussions I've seen about avoiding reincarnation; misinformation about not going to the light. As someone who helps people complete their transition, I can tell you firsthand, this is not helpful advice.

Going to the light is advised if you want a successful transition. Getting stuck in the frequency around the physical world may not be pleasant and it only delays access to available choices, which you will probably like much more.

YOU MUST ASK

Sometimes, I get asked what I consider the most important information I have learned in traveling. I think my answers are probably disappointing to some. Maybe they expect that by learning to do this, some great secrets of the universe get revealed. I try to write about my experiences with the disclaimer that I have no way to validate anything I encounter in these realities, and there is a certain amount of subjectivity that intrudes in all experiences, physical and non-physical. We get information and experiences that conform to our conscious and unconscious programs. It's one thing if I mislead myself; I don't need to be handing out the wrong information to others.

I say this without equivocation; though it is not well known: our free will cannot be impinged upon. I would go out on a limb to say that this is as close to an absolute principle as I have been able to uncover. There is a way, a prerequisite, for the doors of perceptual experience to begin to open and our questions to be answered, and it's incredibly simple. We must ask the questions.

Earnestly asking is a tacit form of permission; it constitutes a conscious choice. Asking big questions is permission in the guise of a request. My first book asks the reader to consider, "Why am I here?". That book was born of the revelation that until we seek the answer to that one, the universe sits waiting for what it has for us. It is possibly the most important question.

In our culture, we are not predisposed to impose on others with our questions, just as I am not inclined to offer advice to anyone about their journey. In that respect, I mimic the guides whom I meet in my travels. When you have a deep yearning to know something or have gotten to the end of your rope around life's circumstances, go into a quiet space, engage your most

HOW TO HAVE A GOOD LIFE AFTER YOU'RE DEAD

sincere emotions, and earnestly ask your questions. I promise you that an answer will come in some form. Pay attention, because it probably won't be in the manner you expect. It may mean you will have to experience change. There may be a disruption to the status quo of your life. Something may disappear that you are particularly attached to. This, too, can be an answer. The timetable is unpredictable, it could unfold slowly over years, or it could be immediate. Some of it depends on how attached we are to not knowing the answer or are reluctant to take the action it requires. It is always up to us. Our choices are treated as sacred. Don't ask if you aren't ready, sometimes there's no going back when that ball gets rolling.

MIKE MARABLE

My Best Assessment

Universe is not only stranger than we think. It is stranger than we can think. – Werner Heisenberg

The more I know, the less certain I become. My best theories have all been extinguished. It would be an abdication of responsibility as a reliable reporter to say that I understand what these experiences mean or how core reality operates. I have provided the best accounting I possibly can and yet I realize it is woefully inadequate. The one thing I know for sure is that our lives—every life—has purpose and meaning. The underlying mechanisms for the reason of any of it is beyond my understanding. I find more questions than answers arise, the deeper I go. It's a trap set by the brain to accept closure on these matters. Our beliefs are rarely accurate, and they can stifle further inquiry.

The observations presented here, and any explanations I have derived from my experiences, are dependent on the same limited equipment that can't find my car keys. You and I may find some consensus and consistency about what we see out in the world because we are part of the same species. A dog, snake or insect will have a very different relationship with their versions of the world. Their headsets allow them to see, hear and smell at levels we can't begin to fathom. We live amongst beings we can't see. We call them dead people, yet they are very much alive and have similar hopes and dreams as you and I. That we ascribe their situation as less desirable is a bias, and, like other biases, they are often misinformed. Some of the dimensions you can't see are far more desirable and interesting than the one you are living in. There are ones where people don't look at their phones for hours each day for example.

The most important message that I hope makes its way out of this book is that you will be around forever. Live as if you are aware that this is the case. Keep building on who you are. Keep living, keep loving and participate in the adventures that are available in this unique learning environment. Some of these can be had through exploring the altered states of OBEs and lucid dreams. People go to the movies to be transported into fantastic stories and beautiful scenery. You can enter three dimensional movies every night where you visit worlds and meet beings that are beyond description. You don't have to wait to die to have these adventures.

When one learns how to turn up the dial and access other frequencies of reality, it is a revelation. We become the fish who figured out how to leave the ocean and walk on land. It increases our options for experience. In any case, you have the opportunity of a lifetime that continues throughout eternity. Strap in for the long ride.

Epilogue

There can be a grace period before we leave this life and move on to the next one. Those of us who aren't leaving just yet may watch someone going through this period with a feeling of sadness. We insert a story reflecting our own grief and caring for someone who may be sick and in decline; heading for what we see as a bleak ending. The person who is leaving may feel this way too. This commiseration can be comforting for everyone in the beginning. There comes a time for dissolving into the experience. We don't want to miss our own dying and what can be learned during this important period. It will be scary, frustrating, and painful along the way. It can also be cathartic and enlightening. Like other parts of living, dying is a mixed bag—not just for the person going through it, but everyone around it.

When you speak with professional caregivers for the dying, they may explain to you that there are stages one can expect to generally unfold throughout the process. These are different for everyone of course, and yet there are similarities. As a society I think we need to be more cognizant of the importance of this period, the time before someone dies, and honor it. There is great opportunity for growth and revelation. It is built into the experience in a condensed form that may have eluded us before.

HOW TO HAVE A GOOD LIFE AFTER YOU'RE DEAD

When our beloved dog Hunter reached the end of his life I knew, and he seemed to know, that he would be leaving us soon. I told my partner we should accommodate his schedule and make him as comfortable as possible while he moves at whatever pace he needs towards his departure. About six months ahead of his leaving I intuitively knew he was getting himself ready. For one, he started visiting me in my dreams more. He was sleeping most of the day and I would watch his legs moving as he dreamed of running and playing. He was beginning his transition and getting used to the environments he would be going to after he moved across the veil.

Hunter came upstairs in his second form one night, his astral body. He slept the night on the floor beside the bed. I found myself in that state as well and reached my non-physical arm over the bed to pet him. Hunter had come to say goodbye. This was one of the ways I knew it was time. About a week after this nighttime visit, one afternoon he got himself up, which was a very difficult task for him at that point and came over to the couch where I was working on this book. He just stood there staring at me. This was unusual. I asked him what he wanted. It was then he let me know he was ready. He had completed his preparation.

Most people don't die suddenly. Those that do may have a more challenging time with closure after they die than folks who are presented the opportunity of moving gently into the good

death. As I have discussed throughout the book, we get clues in advance about our leaving. A sudden increase of dreams about going to the airport or moving to a new location. These can be an indicator of big changes. You might agree that dying is a pretty big change in immediate circumstances. If we pay attention to our inner world, we can get an inkling that we may be closing out this life. These dreams could be about something else entirely but it's still a positive exercise to prepare for our departure ahead of time. It can help get us used to the idea and take some of the sting out of it when it happens. We have also honored it by giving it some thought and consideration; having accepted its inevitability.
Create a sacred space for your transition to unfold. Take advantage of the opportunity it provides for closure and learning. In some ways our whole life is a preparatory grace period for our transition.
-*Mike Marable*

Recommended Books

- Multidimensional Man - *Jurgen Ziewe*
- Vistas Of Infinity - *Jurgen Ziewe*
- Ultimate Journey - *Robert Monroe*
- The Holographic Universe - *Michael Talbot*
- Dreamgates - *Robert Moss*
- Dreamer's Book of the Dead - *Robert Moss*
- Application of Impossible Things - *Natalie Sudman*
- Lucid Dreaming: Dawning of the Clear Light - *Gregory Scott Sparrow, PhD*
- Hand On The Mirror - *Janis Heaphy Durham*
- The Afterlife Of Billy Fingers - *Annie Kagan*
- Surviving Death - *Leslie Kean*
- After - *Bruce Greyson, MD*
- To Heaven and Back - *Mary Neal, MD*
- Farther Shores - *Yvonne Kason, MD*

MIKE MARABLE

HOW TO HAVE A GOOD LIFE AFTER YOU'RE DEAD

Author

Mike Marable is an entrepreneur, activist, writer, and explorer. He is living his best life alongside Gayla, his partner of 19 years, and their dog Hunter near the ocean in Southern California. In 1987 Mike Marable had an extraordinary experience that altered the trajectory of his life. He went searching for answers about what happened to him. This amazing adventure turned into a story that deserves telling. To learn more, visit mikemarable.com

Printed in Great Britain
by Amazon